HANDS

PART ONE

T.L. SMITH

Cover – RBA Design

Photographer - Xram Ragde

Edited – Swish Editing

Editor - Ink Machine Editing & Nice Girl, Naughty Edits

WARNING

This book contains sexually explicit scenes and adult language and may be considered offensive to some readers. This book is intended for adults ONLY. Please store your files wisely, where they cannot be accessed by under-aged readers.

BLURB

She was to be my wife.

I was to be her husband.

Fate had other plans.

She was falling for someone else while I was waiting for her.

When you come from one of the most ruthless families in the country, you're used to getting what you want.

Part of me wanted her, the other...

Well, let's just say, sometimes love can be reckless.

DEDICATION

To all my good girls, who want a man to put her on her knees and tell her what a good, good girl she is. This is for you, my *darling*.

The 'Nice' Brother

Phones have been ringing as the next story is about to
unfold.
We hear the 'nice' brother is to hear wedding bells.
I wonder who the lucky lady will be?

ONE

JOEY

"A bookstore?" I question Keir, my brother.

He shakes his head and gets out of the car, and I follow. We both look inside—the lights are on and the name Pages of Sweets glares back at me.

"Sweets?" I shake my head. "Is that a subtle reference for porn?" I ask. Keir's lip twitches, and he continues walking until we get to the door. "Remind me why we're here?"

Again, he doesn't reply, he simply opens the door. At the same time the bell rings above the door, our heads snap to the back of the store when we also hear a faint noise. My eyes scan the space which isn't much bigger than a small living room, but there are books everywhere.

"What the hell is that?" We both walk farther in, the noise becoming louder with each step.

Is that a... *moan?*

Maybe this is a front for an actual porn shop.

Not only porn books.

Maybe role play?

Okay, now that's a bookshop I want to be a part of—sign me up.

"Oh my God, do not stop."

We both halt as we look up.

A woman with long brown hair flowing over her shoulders, her eyes tightly closed, her hands in someone's hair, her skirt up around her waist as she screams for someone to *not stop* fucking her pussy with their mouth is backed against the wall and one leg over her shoulder.

Just as I see an orgasm take over her body, her eyes pop open. They lock onto mine—

dark whiskey-colored eyes are sightly closed but well aware we're standing here. I don't even spare a glance at the second person until the woman who was getting fucked puts her leg down and smirks. That's when the person who was kneeling between her legs stands. She has short blonde hair cut and styled in a masculine way. The jeans she's wearing hug her tight, showcasing female curves, but her loose shirt would have had me mistaking her for a man from the back at a quick glance.

"This how you treat all your customers?" I ask with a lift of my brow.

The blonde turns around and gasps, wiping at her face before she reaches for a stack of books on the floor and then runs straight past us until we are left alone with the woman with whiskey eyes.

"I feel like whatever you buy now, you should pay extra for the show," she replies, flicking her long hair over her shoulder and adjusting her skirt.

"Not my fault you gave it away for free," I retort.

She pulls a soft smile. It's wary as her eyes lock with mine, but it's gone as she bends down to pick up a pile of books.

"How can I help you? Lucas isn't here," she says, referring to our cousin. How on earth she got involved with him I can't imagine, considering Lucas likes no one.

"You know that's not why I'm here," Keir says, and there's a threatening edge to his tone.

I glance at him, confused, and then back to the woman with whiskey eyes.

Her gaze hardens as she stares at him, lifting her lip in an almost snarl. "I see no reason for you to be here other than for Lucas. So if you don't want to purchase books, it's best you leave."

"I think it's time you closed for the day... wouldn't you say?" Keir is persistent. Not many people argue with him other than his wife.

I watch as she licks her lips, then sucks air between her teeth. "No, I don't think it is." To get past us, she will have to ask us to move or physically shift us herself, as we're blocking her way. She walks up until she's standing right in front of us, then pushes herself between us.

Keir moves, but I stay still.

What the fuck is going on?

"Why are we here?" I ask Keir again.

"You should tell Joey *why* we're here," Keir presses to the brunette.

"Again, if you aren't buying books, you should leave."

"Okay, what the fuck is happening?" I ask Keir and point to the woman. "And who *the fuck* is she?"

Keir heads to the door, but I stay put, still having no clue what is happening.

He looks over his shoulder at me. "That is Adora, your soon-to-be wife," he states, then walks out without another word.

I glance back at Adora as she stands there with

her eyes wide and her mouth slightly open—the shock is written all over her face.

Her stance and expression match mine, I'm sure.

What the fuck?

I'm supposed to marry her.

No way.

No fucking way.

Never!

"You fuck women. No way am I marrying a woman who chooses pussy over my cock."

Adora throws her head back and laughs.

I'm dead serious.

She picks up on my incredulous stare, and her laughter dies down as her eyes find mine. "Oh, you are serious?" She almost whispers the words, but I still hear the amusement in her voice.

"Look..." she steps over and places a soft hand on my chest, and pats it, "... I'm *not* going to be your wife. We both know this. Make your moody boss see it's never gonna happen, will you? Okay, champ?" Adora pats my chest again, this time with more force, then goes to step away, but I reach out and catch her wrist.

"Champ?" My eyebrows rise in another incredulous stare.

She just shrugs as I drop her hand like a hot tamale.

"The way I see it, this..." she waves between us, "... never happened." A slow and steady smirk touches her lips.

"Do you not like cock?" I ask, confused.

"Not yours. Now leave."

"I will *not* under any circumstances marry a woman I will have to convince to sleep with me."

"See, it's settled. Now, can you tell your brother, boss, or whatever you call him?" Adora waves to Keir who's waiting by his car, his face a picture of everything I don't want to see—the stony glare, the upright posture of defiance, and above all, fuck me if there isn't determination in his damn eyes.

"You simply don't tell Keir anything," I mumble.

"I'm sure you're a smart man. Think of something," she responds with a shrug while waving her hand around.

"You also don't lie to him if you want to live," I say, my eyes narrowing into a glare. "Do you know nothing?"

This woman has to know.

Her father is well known. Dangerous. When we were kids, he took his daughter and moved her to Italy when she was ten, and that's the last time I saw her. If I am being perfectly honest, I hardly remember her.

"Where is your father?"

Adora walks behind the counter and stacks a few books before she glances back at me.

"Dead. I killed him," she states.

Then she smiles.

TWO

ADORA

He's cute. Handsome even, but his face is one of utter shock as he looks at me. The sharp angles of his jaw are ticking, and I wonder if that's a sign he's agitated, disturbed, or just plain angry.

"You what?" he asks, apparently not having heard me the first time.

"I killed him."

"Fuck this shit! I'm out." Joey shakes his head and stalks to the door. I watch his retreating back, smiling as he goes.

Maybe I've been avoiding this for no reason at all. I mean, he did get quite the introduction. I would have apologized, but I think it helped my case too. You know, *not* marry someone who I clearly don't want to, and who probably doesn't want me either.

He pauses, his hand on the door.

"How long have you been back?" he asks.

"Years," I answer without hesitation, and he turns back to face me.

"And Lucas knew of this?"

"It took him a while to realize who I was," I tell Joey honestly. "But, yes, he knows who I am."

The woman from earlier pushes the door open, and Joey steps aside, letting her in. She blushes when she sees him and then looks at me.

Dammit! I didn't even get her name.

"Becca," she says, sounding shy, or at least shyer than she seemed a few minutes ago.

Joey looks between us, a smirk touching his lips.

"Yeah, sorry about that." I wave to the door where Joey's watching us.

Becca glances behind her, then nods to the counter. "I left my phone." She walks over and reaches for it, and I place my hand on top of hers. "Do you want my number?" I ask.

I mean, she did just eat me out. Granted, we had only just met when she placed a book on the counter to purchase. Then we got to talking, and one thing led to another, and she ended up with her face between my legs.

What can I say, I have sex appeal.

"You don't want her number."

We both turn to Joey, and I raise a brow at him. Now is not the time for me to make a stand. He ignores my sharp glare and focuses on Becca. "Leave. *Now*."

She snatches her phone from the counter and basically runs past him and out the door.

I bite my tongue. Hard. So hard I can taste blood.

When I glance back at Joey, the front door is closed, and he's standing there with his arms crossed over his chest while he stares at me.

"That's *not* going to happen again." He indicates where Becca just ran out the door.

"You think you can boss me around?"

"I remember you now." His hand runs along the top of my romance books as he slowly approaches the counter. "You and your little sister."

I go to speak, but he cuts me off.

"How is she?" He smirks. "Still breathing?" There is a dare dancing in his eyes. "Let me think! Do I remember correctly? If the deal is not fulfilled, her life will be forfeited. Is that still correct?"

Okay, so I was hoping he wouldn't know about the damn deal.

Joey looks away from me and taps a few times on

his phone before he grins. And the grin that touches his lips is pure evil.

This man is not nice if the vicious glare is anything to go by.

Lucky for me, I'm not nice either.

"This is her, is it not?" He flips his phone, so I can see a picture of my sister with her arm around a boy at her school back in Italy.

My head snaps up as an unholy gasp leaves my mouth.

How did he do that?

How could he possibly know where Abigail is?

I pay for her to go to the best schools—schools where integrity and privacy are assured. He shouldn't have been able to find out where she is or even the name she is using.

"How did you find her?" I ask with curiosity lacing my tone, even though I'm finding it harder to breathe every second with this new information.

"It was you they couldn't find. They never thought to look right under our noses. That was very sneaky of you. But this..." He nods to the phone and pulls it back, sliding it into his pocket. "This was... *stupid*. Did you really think we wouldn't find her?"

"My father signed those contracts. I had nothing to do with them and don't want any part of them."

"Our life doesn't work like that, and you know it. You see, if I don't uphold my contract, that will reflect badly on us as a family. And we can't have that now, can we?"

"You could call it off."

"No, I can't," he replies, leaving no room for argument.

But that doesn't stop me from trying. "You can. You're choosing not to."

"I'm not, actually. I don't want to marry you either." His eyes roam over my body, taking in my long legs in my denim skirt to my midriff top, which shows off my belly and tanned skin, followed by my long brown hair and dark eyes.

"I prefer my women with a bit more meat on their bodies," he remarks with a sinister smile on his lips.

I'm thin, there's no denying that.

Every morning, I run for an hour straight.

Not for physical fitness, but for my mental health. It helps drain out the thoughts that run rampant inside my mind. I started after the first time my father hit me. To get out of the house and away from him I would run—run from him—and before I knew it, hours had passed. Every single time, I would arrive back in a state of exhaustion and simply collapse.

Now the old bastard is gone, but those demons still haunt me. They're not as bad as they were, though. I can breathe out here, now I am away from that life.

I had hoped this day would never come.

I even believed it wouldn't, considering how much time has passed.

But it seems my luck just ran out.

And in walked a tall, dark, and handsome villain.

"You aren't my type either. I mean... you do have a cock, do you not?" I question, pursing my lips in thought simply to annoy him.

"I do. One you would be lucky to have between your legs."

At his words, I can't help but bark out a laugh. "Does that actually work? You saying that women should be pleased to have your cock because it's such a damn gift?" I roll my eyes for good measure.

Joey steps closer and leans down into my face. "No, just you." He smirks.

"Well, I don't feel honored. Actually, I want nothing to do with you..." I glance down at his crotch, "... or your cock," I say with a smile, bringing my eyes back to his as slowly as possible.

"It doesn't matter what *you want*. You *will* be my wife, and you *will not* fight me on this."

"Oh, I won't?"

"No, because I'm sure Miranda would *not* be happy with the outcome."

"You'd take her instead?" I ask, shock evident by my tone, but the look on his face answers my question before he does.

"I would. I mean... when she becomes of age, that is. She's almost eighteen, is she not?"

My hands clench at my sides and my nails dig into my palms. In the fine print of the contract, it states, *should he choose not to end her life, he could take her as his bride.*

That's never going to happen.

When I don't respond, he adjusts his shirt collar and walks back to the door, and without turning around, he says, "I'll see you at six tomorrow for dinner." He pauses and looks back, assessing eyes roaming over me again. "Dress appropriately! I expect the best from my betrothed. Do not come looking like that."

Before I can tell him to go fuck himself, the door slams behind him. I watch as he walks to the car waiting outside, then he gets in and it pulls away.

What the fuck?

Fuck!

I run to the back of the shop and press call on Lucas' contact in my phone. He answers straight away.

"What?"

Isn't he charming?

"Joey knows," I tell him.

Lucas has been covering for me—kind of. Well, he just didn't tell them when he should have. But as he stated, it wasn't his place. I always knew if they'd have asked, he wouldn't have lied, but they never asked.

"When?" he questions.

"Joey just left. Keir brought him in."

"Fuck!" He groans, then I hear some tapping, and he says, "They're coming here."

"I want to run."

"That would *not* be wise," he warns, then hangs up.

THREE

JOEY

"Don't say it." I put the car in drive and speed off. Keir looks up, smirking. "What the actual fuck." I slam my hand against the steering wheel and yell, "I don't want her."

"That isn't your choice," he states simply. I side-eye him as I breeze through a yellow light to get to Lucas.

"You had a choice," I growl, reminding him he was meant to marry someone else, yet he didn't.

"That's different, and you know it," he grumbles.

Yeah, it is. He went through hell with all that. But it worked out for him because he is happily married with kids, and he's madly infatuated with his wife. I guess not all of us can be so lucky.

"I take it you're visiting Lucas," he says as we

come to a stop at his bar. I simply get out of the car, not answering him as I walk to the back door. Before I reach it, it opens to reveal Lucas standing on the other side.

"This is unexpected," Lucas says as he glances past me to Keir, who's still in the car, then back to me. "I see you met your future wife. Did you like her?" he asks, being nothing but a fucking smartass. Which he always is, but right now, I am *not* in the mood.

"How long have you known?" I ask with bite in my tone, not attempting to rein in my frustration.

"A while," he replies in a bored tone that has me clenching my fists before he turns, letting the door go as he steps back inside.

"I should put you in the ground for lying."

"I didn't lie. You never asked."

I suck air through my teeth to stop myself from pulling my gun and aiming it at his fucking head. "You knew she was here, and you never told us."

"Again," he says with a shrug. "You never asked."

"How is Chanel? Should I pay her a visit?"

Lucas moves quickly. One second, he's almost at his desk, the next he's at my throat with a gun aimed at my stomach.

"Drop it, Lucas." Keir's voice rips through the air as he walks in.

Lucas pushes the gun into my stomach, and I smile. "I dare you, asshole," I seethe.

"You do, and I will tear it out of Joey, reload, and you'll get the exact same bullet," Keir warns.

"It would be worth it," Lucas responds, his eyes never leaving mine. No one should underestimate his level of crazy. Lucas gives the gun another push into my gut before he steps back. "Don't fuck with Chanel. Don't even mention her name," he demands.

"He won't," Keir says, ending that discussion.

I actually like his woman. God knows what she sees in this fucked-up lunatic, but it's something none of the rest of us do, that's for sure. And despite the road they took to get where they are, they're happy.

"Lucas, you've been keeping something from us," Keir states, taking a seat at Lucas' desk. He puts his feet up and leans back, locking eyes with Lucas.

"You've seen her," Lucas points out, referring to when he sent Adora to Keir's house to drop off a pair of shoes for Keir's wife, Sailor, when Lucas had pissed Sailor off. Lucas made it up to Sailor by sending Adora out to purchase an incredibly expensive pair of designer shoes for Sailor, which Adora hand-delivered, and Keir just so happened to be there at the time.

"I did, and that's how I worked out who she was," Keir replies. "She is to be married to Joey by the end of next week."

What the actual fuck?

"W-What?" I stutter.

"It stops you from falling in love with someone else, and it closes the deal. Once you're married to her, new shipments will come. I haven't put a push on it because, frankly, we were doing fine the way we were. We took a hit on the last deal when I broke up what was on the table. The families weren't impressed. They will be when they hear of your nuptials to Adora, though."

"She's going to be seething." Lucas almost laughs.

"I... don't... want... to... *marry her*," I tell him, my voice raising with every word as I try not to scream at my brother. My boss.

"Like I said, it must happen soon. I've already booked the church and venue in the car. It's done. It will *not* be undone. I suggest you get used to it." Keir pushes up and stands in front of Lucas. "Hide something like that from me again and I'll kill you. And..." he takes a deep, steadying breath, "... no wife of mine will stop me," he says before he walks out the door.

I turn around and my fist meets drywall, going straight through.

"She isn't *that bad*," Lucas muses. "One of the few women I can actually stand."

"If *you* can stand her, I'm fucked." He chuckles at my words as I pull my hand out of the hole I made in the drywall.

Lucas grabs a bottle of bourbon and pours it over my busted-up knuckles.

"You should tell her... and soon."

"Keir can do it."

"*You* should," Lucas insists. "She's fiery, that one. So be warned." He puts the bottle to his lips and walks off, leaving me standing there with a bloody hand and a fucked-up mind.

FOUR

ADORA

One friend. I have one friend, and that friend is not by choice. But regardless, I love my friend so much.

The problem? I haven't told him anything about who I am. And I really, really need to talk to someone.

"Nope, *nope*, NOPE. Why on earth are you wearing that?" His eyes assess me and the glare he's giving me tells me everything I need to know about my wardrobe choice.

Troy loves fashion and hates it when I don't dress to impress. If he could dress me every day, he would. Without a doubt.

"It's Prada," I say, looking down at my shirt.

"It's nada," he coldly replies, shaking his head as he sits opposite me. "So, why the urgent meeting?

You didn't actually fall in love and plan to get married, did you?"

Ding-dong! He may think he's joking, but how right is he?

"I *am* getting married," I tell him honestly.

"Of course, you are, sweetie. One day soon, when you meet either the perfect man or woman who can keep your interest longer than a one-night stand." He laughs.

"Hey, I slept with Jo twice."

"That's because the second time you were drunk."

"Fine, whatever," I say with an eye roll. "But, Troy..." I bite my lip. "I'm not joking."

"What about, Jo?" he asks.

He's either confused or not really listening—you never know with Troy. He's dressed in a suit with garter belts and bright pink boots. His hair is neatly styled, and his lips shine bright red with lipstick. He looks fabulous. His style is one of the reasons I first spoke to him. I couldn't keep my eyes off him. I'm sure he gets that a lot—actually, I know he does—but I had to approach him and tell him how amazing his style is. His eyes flicked me over, and he said simply, "I know." And ever since then, he's been my best friend. My only friend, really.

"Remember how I told you I came here to escape?" I clutch the coffee in my hand almost to the point of crushing the cup. "Well, no more escaping for me now."

"Has this got something to do with that man who invested in your bookstore? Because we all know Lucas Rossi is bad news. All the Rossis are, honey."

"Yeah, about that—"

"What?"

"I'm meant to be marrying Joey Rossi," I tell him.

He doesn't speak at first, just sits there silently staring at me with his eyebrows crushed together so much they form a single line across his forehead. I think for a moment I might have broken him with my bombshell piece of information.

When he's finally able to respond, he says, "You didn't tell me you were dating. Why would you hide that from me?"

"I saw him yesterday. I haven't seen him since I was ten," I tell him, taking a deep, centering breath. His brows scrunch even further if that's possible as he tries to put it all together in his head. He can't. Believe me, even I can't.

"You're serious," he says, his disbelief evident in his tone.

"Yep. Marrying a Rossi." I smile, only it's not meeting my eyes.

"Fuck, that's a death wish waiting to happen," he jokes, but I realize how serious those words are. "They aren't good men, Adora. Can you not stop the marriage?" he asks.

"No, I have to... I have no choice." My phone starts ringing, and I ignore it, waiting for Troy to speak again. "You'll be there, right? When it finally happens?"

"You like pussy, Adora?"

"I like cock too, you know that. I'm not fussy."

"So you plan to fuck him?"

"No, that is *not* in my plan," I say, shaking my head adamantly.

Fuck my life! I haven't even thought about that possibility. It's probably something I should discuss with him—us seeing other people. I wonder if he'll be good with that.

"Will you answer that phone?" Troy waves his hand in the direction of the incessant ringing. I pull it from my purse and quickly glance down at several text messages, all from *him*.

We need to talk.

Sooner rather than later.

Should I expect to find anyone else between your legs when I see you next?

You wouldn't know what to do with me between your legs. Those screams you gave her would be nothing to what I would give you...

I PULL a face at his message before I switch my phone off.

"Are you mad?" I ask, trying to read his expression. I can't tell if he's amused, horrified, or somewhere in between.

"No, just confused as to why."

"It's arranged and has been since I was a kid. It's something I can't say no to. Please believe me when I say that."

His pink nails tap on the table... once, twice, three times. "You haven't lied to me before, and I hope you aren't starting now. So, yes, I believe you."

"Thank you."

"Doesn't mean I have to like him." He smirks.

"No, you don't. I'm not even sure I like him." I smirk back, making him laugh.

"Oh, gosh, this is going to be *so good.*"

"If you say so." I shrug, not believing a word coming from his mouth.

———

"DO YOU EVER ANSWER YOUR PHONE?" I jump at the sound of the voice as I enter my apartment, and a scream rips from my throat. Clutching my bag, I quickly scan the area and find Joey leaning up against my counter, his phone in hand and his eyes on me.

"Do you usually break into people's apartments?" I bite back.

Closing the door, I approach the other side of the kitchen counter and face him. He slides his phone into his pocket and locks eyes with me. Icy blue eyes stare at me. I've seen that shade of blue once before, when I was visiting Thailand and went to the Phi Phi Islands. The crystal-clear water with hints of blue, the color is exactly what his eyes remind me of.

"If you'd answer your phone, you would have known I was trying to be respectful of your time by arranging a time to speak. But since you chose to ignore all my calls and text messages, here I am." He throws his hands out at his sides, indicating that he is indeed here.

A bit dramatic, I think.

"How did you even find out where I live?"

"It was easy once I knew who I was looking for."

I turn, giving him my back as I move to the refrigerator and pull out a bottle of water. "That's what a stalker does."

He bites his bottom lip, and I must remember I don't like this man because he looks way too good doing that.

"We need to talk."

"Talk! Ah-huh, since you broke in and all." I smile. "Or leave! Yeah, that would be better, so I can change the locks."

"You won't be living here much longer, so changing the locks would be a waste of everyone's time."

While I digest his words, I stare at him blankly. "Where will I be living?" I ask, confused.

"With me, of course." He says it so easily, so clearly, so precisely...

I want to run.

"Of course, what was I thinking. Do I get any

sort of say in this?" I steady my breathing because, unfortunately, I already know the answer.

"I don't believe you do."

"Is that all you came to say?" I nod to the door. "Because you can show yourself out."

"No. Actually, I came to tell you our date."

"Date?" I huff. I am more than ready for him to get out of my space.

"Yes, of when we're getting married."

"I don't care about dates. Just text it to me."

"It's next week," he states nonchalantly.

I swear my soul has left my body.

It's drifting somewhere in outer space.

My mind has gone with it.

I thought I would have time.

Maybe get myself out of it somehow.

Some way.

But now I see that's not an option.

When I finally look up at Joey, he's been watching me, assessing me, as he waits for me to finally speak and when I don't, he says, "The bridal shop has my card. Go there and pick what you need." He moves to walk past me, but I stop him with a hand to his chest.

That was a mistake.

I realize it the minute my hand touches him.

I pull it away quickly, bringing it back to my side.

His brow scrunches at the brief contact.

"I don't need your money."

"Why?" he asks.

"I have my father's. How do you think I pay for Abigail's schooling?" I say, referring to my sister. "I probably have more money than you."

"So why did Lucas need to buy into your little bookshop, then?"

I scoff at his choice of words, *my little bookshop*.

"I was still waiting for the money to come through when I met him, and it seemed like a good fit. Lucas is a good man."

Joey throws his head back and laughs. His hands clutch his stomach as his laughter picks up and becomes louder and louder.

I cross my arms over my chest as I wait for him to finish.

I hate to say it, but his laugh is attractive.

How is that possible?

For a laugh to be attractive?

I'm not even sure.

I don't like this man, not one bit. And if I had a choice, I would *never* marry him. I've seen what marriage does to people, and it's not good, that's for sure.

His gaze drops to find mine again, and his crystal-clear blue eyes narrow as his laughter abruptly stops. "Lucas is anything but a good man, even his girl knows that."

"I like Chanel," I remark, smiling.

"Seems you have terrible taste. Not in Chanel, but definitely in Lucas. Lucas is the worst of us, and that's saying something. Stay away from him." He steps past, leaving me standing there with my mouth hanging open in disbelief.

"You will not, not for a single second..." I seethe, stomping toward him, and as he stops and turns back to me, my finger jabs into his chest, "... think you can tell me who and what I can and can't be around. You are *not* my father, and even if you were, look where that got him," I add with a smile. "I'll slit your throat in your sleep if you think you can tell me what to do." I remove my finger and step back, gesturing toward the door. "You can leave now. Have a nice night, Joey." A small smirk tugs at his lips, but he doesn't move a muscle. "I said... *you can leave now.*"

"No. I have a better idea. Why don't you come to mine so you can see your new room?"

"All the better to slit your throat in?" I taunt.

"See, the more you talk dirty to me, the more I want to fuck you." The smirk he has firmly ingrained on his face hasn't left, and I don't know if he's serious or not. "A little blood never hurt no one." He shrugs, and my stomach flips. "Get a coat and let's go." He pulls open my front door and takes a few steps. When he notices I'm not following, he stops. "You have ten seconds, or I will spend the night here in your bed."

I would like to say I think he's joking, but I have a feeling he isn't. So, somewhat reluctantly, I grab my coat and keys, then follow him out as I lock my front door. We walk down to his car, and he doesn't open my car door for me.

Pig!

I scoff at him as I do it myself.

"What?" he says.

"You are no gentleman, Joey Rossi." I get in, pulling the coat over me before I buckle myself in.

"And you ain't no lady. So let's not get too tied up in what we are now, shall we?"

It's wrong to hit him in the head with my phone, right?

Or stab him in the neck with my keys?

I could do either and smile while doing it. Instead, I sit here, not saying a word, as he drives. And he doesn't say anything either.

Asshole.

FIVE

JOEY

She smells like bubble gum with hints of cotton candy.

Why the fuck does she smell so good?

It makes me so mad.

No woman should smell *that* good.

Especially not her.

She sits rigidly in the passenger's seat, her phone and keys clutched in her hand. I'm pretty sure she wants to stab me with them.

That's not going to happen.

I pull up to my house, and her nose turns up.

"Does it have to be so flashy?"

I glance back at my home, a brownstone with three stories right near Keir's.

"It's not flashy. Now get out."

She follows as I stride up the stairs to the front door. Her footsteps are heavy as I push the black door open. Adora comes in behind me, and I feel her scrutinizing glare taking everything in.

"You like the color blue," she states.

"I do," I reply as Adora walks into the kitchen and runs her hands over the white marble countertop with a blue backsplash. Black stools sit on one side of the counter and black pendant lights drip from the ceiling. The sliding glass door next to the kitchen leads out to a small outdoor sitting area.

Adora walks to the left and continues her investigation, stopping when she gets to the back of the house. I stare in fascination as her hands run along my books.

She glances back at me. "You need some romance in your life," she comments as she looks over the titles. "This is all law and finance."

"I enjoy them."

She laughs under her breath, then gets to the white library ladder which sits in front of the blue shelving. She turns, sitting her ass on it, and looks up at me as the downlights highlight the books behind her.

"I hate it," I can hear the lie as she says it.

"You can put your romance books there." I point to a shelf, and she tries to fight her smile, but it wins.

"Really?" she asks.

"Yes."

"What about the color?" Chocolate-colored hair flicks across her face as she glances behind her to the shelving.

"The blue stays."

"I guess I can work with that." She shrugs, then shoots me a glare straight from the pits of Hell. "I'm not fucking you. You having my body never was, and never will be, a part of this arrangement."

"If you say so." I lift a brow, smirking.

"I'm not joking. That's a hard no."

I refrain from rolling my eyes.

"You need to have a bridesmaid. Keir will be my best man."

"My only friend is a guy. I guess he'll wear a dress for me, though."

I don't even bother arguing with that statement.

"You can take me home now."

"Wrong. This is your home now. Would you like to get your shit tonight or in the morning?" I ask, changing the plans.

"No, I'm not living with you until after we're married," she bites back. "And, so help me God, if you threaten my sister again, I will castrate you in your sleep."

"I thought you weren't going anywhere near me. How can you castrate me if you refuse to touch me?"

Adora climbs off the ladder and saunters over to me. "You have a sidepiece, do you not?" she asks, her whiskey eyes not leaving mine.

"Of course," I tell her, even though I'm not sure where she's going with this question.

"Well, I have many sidepieces, so let's keep it that way." She waves a finger between us. "And this can be a simple business transaction." She smiles, and I grind my teeth.

"None of your fucks are allowed into my house," I bark at her, trying to keep my voice even, showing I am not losing my cool.

"That goes for you as well. This house... *your* house, as you put it... is a no-go for your little hoes too."

"Deal," I say, sealing it with a firm nod.

"Good. Now, I get to choose the color for your suit."

I start shaking my head, but she purses her lips, cutting me off. "Blue. You can be my something blue."

"Done."

"And—"

"You don't get to make demands in this situation," I cut her off.

Her lashes flutter as she looks at me with a devilish smile. "Oh, but I do. Isn't it fun to do this? Can you wear something pink for me?"

"Then you will wear something red for me," I reply, crossing my arms over my chest.

"Like?" She mimics my movement, crossing her arms, her finger tapping her lips in mock interest.

"I'll think of something, don't worry."

"I am worried. I see your imagination, and it's dull... very dull." She spins on the spot, taking in all the books again, her hair whipping around her as she does. "I want this room."

"I told you, you can have it." I start pacing back and forth.

"I want my own bedroom as well." It's not a request from her lips, more like an order.

"No. You will sleep in my bed," I tell her firmly, watching as she continues to look over every book's spine.

"I am not going to fuck you." Her head turns to spare me a glance, that smirk now firmly back in place. She thinks this is funny, but it irritates the fuck

out of me. Then she looks away as if I am mean-
ingless.

Walking over to her, I bend down so I am close to
her ear. "You will. It's just a matter of time." I watch
as goosebumps litter her skin.

"*If you say so,*" she singsongs.

SIX

ADORA

After last night, I found my own way home, and convinced him I can get my shit myself. Even though he insisted he'd take me, I figured it was best he didn't. It's a lot to take in, considering I had thought I had gotten away with it all. Not having to fulfill the contract, keeping Abigail safe from this life—I was wrong.

If he hadn't found out about Abigail, I would have fought him tooth and nail. Unfortunately, that didn't happen. I love my little sister, and the best thing I ever did was get her out of that place.

The bell over the door jingles, and Lucas enters with Chanel by his side. She walks straight over to me and gives me a quick cuddle before she wanders off to the dark romance books. Which is ironic since she is basically living one of her very own. She's grown to love the genre, though, thanks to Lucas.

"Seems you have been pissing off Joey," Lucas remarks, straight-faced, but I can hear it in his voice that it makes him happy.

"He does that *all by himself*," I retort, smiling.

"Oh, I have no doubt. So you said yes to the big day, even after you told me that it would never happen."

"He found my sister," I tell him.

"Joey is good at finding people, which makes me wonder why he never looked you up." Chanel places a book on the counter. Lucas eyes it, then asks me, "Which kink will I be expected to experiment with tonight?" Chanel blushes as I pick up the book.

"This one is cutting," I answer, and Lucas shakes his head.

"You are not to shed a single fucking drop of blood, do you understand?" Lucas says as Chanel takes the book from me.

"Thanks. If you get any new ones, can you hold them for me?" She hands me cash, even though she doesn't have to. Lucas puts money into the business and barely takes any out. He takes a few books every couple of months. Now it's Chanel, but she pays every single time.

"Will do."

"Adora…" We all turn to see Becca standing there, phone in hand and short blonde hair pushed back. She's dressed in tight jeans and a fitted pink shirt, which shows a bit of cleavage.

"You must be the one who was between Adora's legs," Lucas comments, and Chanel hits him in the stomach. He grunts and shrugs.

Becca's face goes bright red as she looks toward the door, then back to me. "Can we talk?"

I give her a slight nod before Chanel pulls Lucas out the door. When they're gone, Becca steps up to the counter, and her delicate hands touch the countertop. Her nails are painted pink to match her shirt.

"What's up?" I ask, confused as to why she's here.

"Look, I don't normally do this, or even what we did the other day…" She glances back at the bookshelf where she ate me out. "But I wanted to know if you would like to go on a date with me."

"You want to *date* me?"

"Yes, if you would be willing."

"But…" My brows pinch together. "I've got all kinds of issues. I'm not sure you really want to."

Her green gaze falls to her hands. "I do, though. I like you."

"You don't know me."

"This is true, but I can see that you're pushing through this thing we call life just the same as I am."

"Becca, you are beautiful... stunning even. Are you sure you want this? You could go and find a normal, healthy girl to take you on a date. Trust me when I say that would be better for you. My life..." I shake my head. "It's about to get real messy."

"No."

"No, what?"

"No, I would not like to find someone else. I have a connection with you that I have never had with anyone else. I did something I would never have done in a million years because it felt right. You made me feel these things are right, when all my life I was raised to believe they are wrong. This isn't wrong." She waves between us as she finishes speaking.

I feel butterflies take flight in my stomach. What's the worst that could happen?

"Okay, but you can't say I didn't warn you."

"Tonight?" she asks, a smile edging on her beautiful lips.

"Sure," I reply, shrugging. She hands me her phone, and I type in my number before handing it back to her. Then she rings it, and my phone lights up.

"Now you have mine." Her smile is contagious as she walks to the door, then looks back. "Should I pick you up?"

"No. Just tell me where and when, and I'll make my own way there." She nods before she leaves, shutting the door behind her.

I'm not sure this is a good idea, but I didn't want to say no either.

SHE'S DRESSED in a hot pink dress that stops just above her knees and a pair of black heels. Her hair is styled pretty much the same way it was when I saw her earlier, but now she's wearing pink lipstick. Her green eyes spot me as I move closer. I have on a pair of jeans, knee-high boots, and a cropped white shirt. My hair is down, and I even ran the straightener through it.

"You look beautiful," she says, leaning in, her soft lips touching the side of my cheek before she pulls back.

"You do as well."

Her cheeks flush, matching the color of her lips.

"Am I your first girl date?" I ask, my curiosity taking over.

She turns, walks to the restaurant door, and holds it open for me to enter. "You are. Does that bother you?"

"No, not at all. I usually don't date. So firsts all around."

"But I wasn't your first woman, was I?" she asks, and her assumption is spot on.

"No, you are for sure not." I laugh.

"Are you bisexual?" she asks, then shakes her head. "I mean, sorry, that was rude of me." She quickly turns to the hostess and gives her name before we are escorted through to a table for two.

"I am, and you?"

"I like guys, but I like you more."

"You don't even know me," I say, her interest in me after just one encounter makes my mind whirl.

"I get vibes, and your vibe is amazing. I like to be around you. It's why I did what I did. I would have never done that in other situations."

"What, randomly hook up?" I chuckle as we sit.

"Yes. The last woman I was with it was secret, we never dated nor went anywhere in public. We were on and off for years. We were best friends, which didn't work out. I wish her well, but she wasn't it. You are the only other woman I've been with in a long time."

"I've been with many women and men," I tell her honestly. "I haven't done relationships."

"I like that you said you haven't done... that means you're open to it." She smiles, and I immediately feel a bit guilty. The waiter comes back right as I'm opening my mouth to elaborate. She orders a bottle of wine as he pours our water, and as soon as he leaves, I decide to put it all out there.

"I have to tell you something." I put the menu down. "I'm getting married in a week."

She lowers her menu, placing it gently in front of her, and looks at me in shock with those big green eyes.

"I..." She shakes her head. "I don't understand. You don't wear a ring." Her gaze falls to my hand. "Why would you agree to go on a date with me if you're getting married?" she asks in disbelief.

"Because it's not my choice. If I had a choice, I wouldn't marry him."

"It's your family?" she asks.

"Yes, you could say that."

"Oh, I'm so sorry." She reaches across the table and touches my hand, giving it a squeeze. "I know the pressure of parents. Mine don't believe in same-sex marriage. They ignore me when I tell them I like women, they do not approve. So I get it."

"I have to look at dresses tomorrow."

"I can come," she suggests, surprising me.

"You want to come while I pick out a dress to marry someone else?"

She shrugs like it's no big deal.

But it is.

"I mean, I'm not opposed if it means spending more time with you."

"I'm not a good catch. I want you to know that before we go any further."

"Is anyone?" She raises a brow, and I find myself smiling at her answer.

"I'm sure many people are. A beautiful woman like yourself could find a normal woman, not someone who is destined to marry a man she doesn't like, let alone love."

"I want to give it a try, don't you?" She shrugs. "As I said, I've never met anyone like you before, and I like you. I like your attitude, the way you hold yourself, it's comforting and welcoming."

If only she knew about my demons.

The dinner goes well. She makes me laugh. I make her laugh. We bond over everything pink. She tells me about her French Bulldog named Beyoncé, which also makes me laugh. *Who names their dog after a singer?* I guess she does.

She tells me about her first love—a woman—who was also her best friend.

I tell her I've never been in love.

It's not a lie.

She asks to kiss me at the end of the night as we walk to our cars, so I reach out and grab her by the hips and pull her to me.

She giggles.

It's perfect.

Lips as soft as velvet touch mine, and it's in that moment that I wonder if what I'm doing is right. So why, when I kiss her, does my brain go straight to a brooding, demanding, tattooed asshole?

I hate him.

"I want to invite you back to mine," she whispers against my lips. "But I have work tomorrow. And I know if I do, we'll be awake all night." She giggles again.

How can I attract someone so... nice?

But then, there is Joey.

"I have to pack anyway," I tell her.

She smiles and leans in and kisses my lips one more time, lingering as she does. "Tonight was quite perfect." Her hands leave me and drop to her sides.

"It was. Not sure why I always say no if it's meant to be like this."

We stop at a car that's red, sporty, and looks expensive.

"What do you do for work? Can't believe I haven't asked you that." I shake my head, pushing my hair over my shoulder.

"I'm a lawyer," she replies, smiling.

Wow! Okay. I did not expect that.

"I wanted to ask you something..." She opens her car door and places her purse on the seat. "Those men that were at your shop, the ones who walked in on us. Who are they?"

"One of them will soon be my husband." I bite my lip as I wait for her reaction.

"Oh." Her mouth forms an O as she nods. "I know who they are."

"You do?" I ask, my eyes widening.

"I did some digging when I left the bookstore. They have quite the reputation."

"They do," I agree.

"Dangerous," she adds, her eyes connecting with mine.

"Yep." I slide my hands into the back pockets of my jeans.

"And you're safe... being around them?"

Safe? Mmm... not sure how to answer that.

"Yep," is all that leaves my mouth. I point to my car and tell her I'll talk to her later.

She appears disappointed by my abrupt departure, but someone is standing by my car who looks awfully familiar.

SEVEN

JOEY

There's no way I was following her, but here she is. Standing in front of me, looking like sex on a damn stick. Her knee-high boots and tight-ass jeans fit her perfectly. Her tongue darts out, and she licks her lips, eyeing me for an explanation.

"You adding stalker to your list?" She crosses her arms over her chest. She has small tits, but the gesture perks them up just a little.

"This is one of our restaurants," I tell her. "I was coming to take payment and pick up food." She doesn't move as I step closer. "Join me." I keep walking, and she follows behind as I go through the back door, the kitchen hand nodding his head in greeting as I enter. The chef gives me a small wave as his face pales.

"Do you get off on making people scared of you?" she whispers.

"They aren't scared of me. They're scared of what happens if they don't make payment. It's as simple as that. You pay, there's no issue." I shrug.

"Fuckhead."

I almost want to laugh at her words, they're so vulgar, but I like it.

"How was your date?" She steps closer while everyone in the kitchen moves around us as we wait at the end of the counter the chef is using.

"Who said I was on a date?" she bites back. She pushes her hair behind her ear, sucking her lip between her teeth as she rolls it.

"Are you telling me you weren't? That was the same woman you were fucking in your bookstore, was it not?"

She scans the area and sees a few eyes on us.

I don't care, it's none of their business.

"Yes, it was her."

"You told her you're marrying me?" I ask, just to be sure.

"I did," she answers as the chef comes over and slides a plate in front of me.

I look down at it and smile. "Chef, this looks amazing."

"This one is a bit different than last time. It has specks of honeycomb throughout. I'm gonna add it tomorrow if you say it's good."

Adora looks at the chef. "Why do you care what he thinks of your cake?" she asks.

The chef looks at me, and I simply give him a small nod, which she doesn't see as he continues to talk, "Joey, here, has the best palate for anything sweet. Maybe not savory, but sweet he knows." He chuckles.

Adora's eyes find mine as I take the first bite. It's a mixture between a mud cake and a brownie—the honeycomb giving it an out-of-this-world texture.

"Best one yet," I tell him, which earns me a smile.

"I was hoping so." I offer the fork I just used to Adora, and her brows pinch together as she looks at it. She's hesitant but slides the fork through the dessert before bringing it to her lips. I watch as the flavors hit her, and she moans loudly and almost falls as her eyes spring open.

Adora eagerly nods her head. "I don't agree with *anything* this man says, but this is amazing." She goes to take another bite.

"Why thank you, kind lady." The chef bows before he walks off.

I remain where I am, watching her demolish the cake. She eats the rest, not offering me another bite. When she's done, she smiles wide. "Now that's a cake you could fuck to."

"Fuck to?"

"Yeah, you know. You're in the middle of fucking and you want to add some extra flavor, that cake is your girl."

"I'll keep that in mind." I remove the plate from her hand. "In case you embarrass yourself and try to lick it clean."

Adora's hands fly to her hips. "I was planning on licking it clean. I'm pretty good with my tongue."

"I'm sure you are."

The chef walks back and holds out a box of cake. "For you, miss."

She takes it, smiling gratefully, and peeks inside. "Thank you so much."

"You're sharing that with me," I tell her.

Her stare is hard as she locks eyes with me. "That's a hard no." Then she turns and walks back to the door.

The manager comes through and hands me an envelope, but I don't stay and talk. Instead, I walk straight out after Adora.

"I want to go tomorrow," I tell her, and she stops halfway to her car.

"You what?" she asks, sounding confused as she turns around to look at me.

"I want to go tomorrow."

"No, you aren't allowed." She shakes her head vehemently, and it makes me want to laugh.

"I don't think we're really following any sort of traditions," I argue.

"I don't want you there. It's as easy as that."

"Why not?" I press, and her shoulders lift with a deep breath.

"Because I don't." Her lips thin.

"You don't have any family with you. Your only family is in Italy attending a boarding school. So unless you plan to put her on the next flight straight away, I'm your only option apart from your friend."

"You aren't my *only* option." She smiles, but it's not nice.

"So, you've invited your date, then?" Her smile falters, and she sucks air between her teeth. "I see..." I chuckle, turning her fake smile into a glare.

"You are a real ass, you know that?" she bites out. "Is this who you are? You read people?" She steps up closer, and I want to lean in and wrap my hands around her neck. Then I want to kiss the shit out of her.

Whoa? Where the fuck did that come from?

"You are the easiest to read, even if you try the hardest to hide it." I grin and walk back to my car. "I'll be seeing you tomorrow."

"Do *not* come," she yells out after me.

EIGHT

ADORA

I've been on edge all morning. I opened the bookstore, then came here to meet Becca. She's dressed more casually today in jeans and a leather biker jacket. When she sees me, she leans in for a kiss, but I only give her my cheek.

It's easy to see her confusion when she pulls back.

"Sorry, it's a crazy day." I shake my head.

"Do you want me to go?" she asks, and I hate that I hesitate to respond.

How badly I want to tell her yes.

I glance around and don't see him anywhere.

Hopefully, he doesn't show.

Now that's wishful thinking, isn't it?

"No, it's fine." I pull open the door, and a lady

greets us, handing us two glasses of champagne as we walk in, and tells us to take a seat while she brings out a rack of dresses.

"The notes request white," she comments at my confusion as I look at the dresses.

"Yes, that's correct," a deep voice I instantly recognize says from behind us, and my heart feels like it stops before it starts racing. Joey walks in and steps around where I can see him clearly. He turns to Becca and offers his hand. "You must be the side-piece." I hear a loud gasp of surprise from the bridal lady as Becca offers him her hand. I watch as her cheeks pinken at the sight of him.

He's nice to look at, there's no doubt about that.

Joey is handsome, rugged, and downright delicious. That mixture has you wanting him to call you a good girl or spank you hard for having an attitude. And I always seem to have an attitude with him, so I guess I'm in the latter category.

But it's the way he watches and takes everything in.

He knows your moves before you do.

He can read you better than anyone else can.

Joey is an observer.

I'm sure he's just as dirty as his brother and cousins. He is, after all, second-in-command to his brother, Keir, and he wouldn't have that if he wasn't good at what he does.

And that's as intimidating as it is deadly.

His smile is deceiving.

Conniving.

Calculating.

"I don't want white."

Joey grabs my glass of champagne and sits down beside me. So now I'm in the middle of Becca and him.

"I want to see you in white."

"No."

"I'm paying. Try the dress on, Adora."

"Fuck you!" I snap back at him.

"Does she have this foul mouth with you as well?" Joey asks, addressing Becca.

"No," she answers quietly.

"You don't have to answer him," I tell her but keep my eyes on him.

"She can answer me. Don't control her," Joey says, his tone taunting.

"You are the only asshole being controlling." I get up from my seat. "I'll try one white dress on, then you have to leave," I tell him, my hands landing on my hips.

"Two," he argues back.

Turning around to the bridal lady, I smile at her. "Pick me two to try on so we can pick the *real dress* and *he* can leave."

"Is that your fiancé?" she almost whispers.

"Yes. Isn't he an ass?"

Her eyes go wide, and she isn't sure how to answer that. Instead, she gets busy putting two dresses into the changing room as I follow her in. The first is a tight lacy one with a small train. It's beautiful, classic, and quintessential.

I walk out, and both sets of eyes lock on me.

"Wow!" Becca breathes out, and Joey's eyes take me in before he turns to her. "Is this not weird for you? You're helping a woman you are fucking pick a wedding dress for the man she's marrying."

For fuck's sake, I want to walk over to him and slap him hard.

The bridal lady excuses herself and hurries away.

Who could blame her?

"Joey," I snarl as Becca stands to leave. "Don't leave. He's being an ass." She pauses, and I glare at him. "One more dress and you *will* leave."

I stalk back into the changing room and start taking off the dress as the bridal lady enters and silently helps me. When I have the next one on, I walk out to Becca facing the other way and Joey watching her with a smirk.

"Last dress, *now leave.*"

Joey gets up, true to his word, and walks over to me. "It's been a pleasure," he says and nods, then walks out the door.

Becca smiles when she turns and sees me.

"Do you plan to ever get married?" I ask her.

"No, my family would not attend."

"Would it be weird if you came to mine?" Again, I can feel the bridal lady staring at us.

"I would love to."

"Good! Done deal." I go back to the changing room and smile at the bridal lady, who we are providing with at least a month's worth of gossip.

"Now, get me something in red."

Her eyes go wide, but she remains silent.

Good woman.

HE HASN'T ANNOYED me for two days, and the wedding day is creeping up on me.

But Becca, I've seen her every day. We haven't gone further than kisses to the lips, and I'm okay with that. I have so much going on that I'm not really sure it was smart to start something with her to begin with.

The problem is, I just can't seem to tell her that, though.

Her energy, who she is as a person, is sweet, and that energy draws you in. I'm not used to being around someone like her. I'm so broken and fucked-up that it's refreshing.

Joey is the same as me, we are two peas in a pod, really.

"I heard you're having a bachelorette party tonight." I turn my head to see Lucas on the other side of the counter. The store isn't even open yet, but he has keys.

"No, who said that?"

"Joey's bachelor party is tonight, so I assumed you were having yours with only two days until the wedding." I cringe at the reminder. "There is a way out of this, just so you know."

This piques my interest. I turn my body, giving him my full attention. "And what is that?"

He shakes his head. "I'm not sure you want the answer."

"I do," I argue back.

He steps up closer, just a few inches from me. To all others, Lucas is one of the most feared men. It's all part of his beauty, and you can see it if you look closely enough. It's incredibly dark under those hypnotic eyes.

"I can kill you. It's been a while since I've had my hands around another woman's neck. Not sure Chanel would approve, but I'm happy to assist."

I shake my head at his words and give him an eye roll.

"Go to hell, Lucas." I turn back to stacking the bookshelf.

"I've already been, and the Devil himself kicked me out," he jokes. "Okay, since that's not an option, I've been instructed to tell you that the girls expect you at nine tonight." I raise a brow and glance over my shoulder at him. "I mean, my offer still stands." He smirks.

"Why?"

"Fucked if I know." He shrugs.

"Why are you here?" It's not like him to pop in all the time. He hardly used to, it was always his right-hand man. But since he was shot dead in this store, Lucas hasn't replaced him.

"I own this place as much as you," he replies simply.

"Chanel is working, and you're bored, right?" I put two and two together. His face betrays nothing, but I know I'm right. "You could go and hang with your boss and his brother," I joke.

"No, I'd rather slit my wrists than hang with your soon-to-be husband."

His words make me laugh rather loudly.

"Whose throat are you slitting?"

We both turn to the sound of Joey's voice.

Fuck me.

"I'm out."

"Should I be worried that you spend so much time with my fiancée?" Joey asks Lucas as he passes him, and Lucas glances over his shoulder at me. "More than likely."

I know he's joking, he said that to piss off Joey. Lucas nods to me before he walks out.

"We're closed. Did you not read the sign?" I turn back and face the bookshelves, giving him my back— exactly what he deserves.

"Is that the way you greet all your customers? It's a touchy time for bookstores these days. You would think you should be welcoming me."

"We do just fine, thank you very much."

"So, you have money?"

"I do." I turn my head and smile at him.

"So why don't you buy Lucas out, then?" he questions.

"Because he's a great business partner," I argue. I haven't really thought of changing things because I'm happy with the way they are. I'm even planning on hiring someone else to give me more time off.

"We should kiss."

My hand pauses on a book that is full of stories about single dads finding love. I focus on the cover as I think over what he's just proposed. *How do I answer that?*

"Adora."

Upon taking a deep breath, I slide the book in its place and turn to face him. "You should read a book," I tell him.

What was that? I'm not sure why I even said it. But it was better than telling him to get fucked. I'm not going to lie, I want to know what he kisses like, but am I ready for that?

"We have to kiss on our wedding day. Would you rather not get our first one out of the way beforehand?"

He has a valid point, but...

"No, thank you," I manage to say but don't fully mean it. "I don't plan to kiss you on that day either."

"You have to," he replies. "We're marrying in a church, and you will kiss me."

He's right, I know he is, but I still want to argue the point with him.

"I can't. Sorry, I'm busy."

He takes two large steps until he is in front of me, then his calloused hand grasps my chin and lifts it.

I let him, watching in fascination. I'm stuck in a moment of time where I am contemplating the whole *should-I-or-shouldn't-I* dilemma.

As he leans in, his lips coming closer, now would be the perfect time to stop him.

To tell him to fuck off, to not kiss me because I don't want him.

However, that's a lie.

We all know it.

I want to know what it's like to kiss him.

If you had asked me that question over a week ago, I would have told you quite the opposite.

This is *not* instalove.

Hell, I don't even know if I actually like the man.

But that doesn't mean his lips aren't full enough that I haven't dreamed about how they would feel on my lips and how they would feel everywhere.

I'm a kisser.

I love to be kissed.

On every part of my body.

Anywhere and everywhere.

And girls kiss the best.

No man has ever kissed me so passionately that my head has spun, and I wondered what it would be like to never kiss them again.

Joey's lips touch mine, and instantly I taste oranges. What a weird flavor. It's as if he just bit into one, and now he's sharing it with me. His lips move softly against mine, languidly.

Well, well, well! Who knew he could kiss like that?

He's not hard nor demanding like I thought he would be. Instead, he's gentle yet still domineering.

I like it.

My mouth opens, and he takes that opportunity to slide his tongue inside, and the minute he does, my head whips back as I come to my senses, and I break our kiss.

"Done! Now we only have to do that one more time and never have to do it again." I smile and walk away from him as fast as my feet will allow me.

When I step into the back office, I check the security cameras to see if he's still there, but he's gone. And that's when I finally breathe.

But what lingers is the taste of oranges.

Touching my lips, I try to think of why I hate oranges and come up with nothing.

NINE

JOEY

I kissed her.

I kissed her, and she's a temptress.

I kissed her, and I want more.

If she hadn't broken that kiss, I would have held her to me and tasted every inch of her luscious body. I was tempted from the beginning.

"No sex club!" Sailor yells as we walk out the door.

Keir looks back at her and raises a brow.

"What? I know what happens there. That's where you found me." She winks and walks up the stairs.

"We are so going to a sex club," Piper says, huffing out a laugh.

"You should be with the girls," I tell her.

Piper places a hand on her hip, and Keir says nothing because he actually likes her. Yes, she's our cousin, but she listens to him without argument and that's something Keir demands—loyalty, respect, reverence.

"I'm with you guys."

"Piper." Keir turns to face her.

She simply rolls her eyes and goes back inside.

Angelo, one of our third cousins who isn't so much in this life but runs one of our many businesses, is with us. "Lucas will meet us there."

I say nothing as we get into the car.

"You think you'll be happy with her?" Keir asks, his expression unchanging. Always hard and uncompromising.

"Is anyone happy with someone they don't choose to marry?" I reply.

"Yes, and you know it."

"Our mother was never happy. Our father was a power-hungry dick." He's well aware of this fact, since he is the one who ended up having to deal with our father.

"That was a different scenario."

"You never married who you were meant to," I point out. *Again*.

"Joey."

"I'm just saying... you found a way out of it, why can't I?" I look to Angelo, who has been silently taking in our exchange. "You want to marry a fiery little thing that reads romance books all day?"

"Married." He holds up his hand, showing his wedding band.

"I hear two wives is where it's at."

He laughs at me, but Keir does not.

"What do you want to drink?" Keir opens the bar in the limo and pulls out a bottle of bourbon. I snatch it from him, twisting the lid and chugging as much as I can before I feel the need to throw up.

"My future wife also likes pussy. Who knew that was a possibility?" I fake laugh, the whiskey is talking for me now.

Angelo sits there, stunned into silence, and Keir merely shakes his head at me.

"Who even knows if she likes dick. But she ain't touching this dick since she's still fucking that little blonde."

"Tell her to stop," Keir says, looking at me like I'm dense since this is the obvious solution.

"No, because I plan to fuck whoever I want as well. So how would that be fair if I demanded that of her?"

"We don't deal in fair," Keir states simply.

"I kissed her today."

"And..." Keir asks as I put the bottle back to my lips and take another two large mouthfuls, the burn slowly moving down until I don't feel it anymore.

"She tastes like cinnamon," I answer, my brows pinched.

"And that's bad?" Angelo asks, and I swallow past the growing lump in my throat.

"It's fucking terrible," I say.

Because I want to taste more—but I don't tell them that.

Keir's phone rings, and he answers it straight-away. When he hangs up, I'm already halfway through the bourbon and well on my way to passing out and forgetting about tonight and that kiss.

"Seems your fiancée hasn't shown up," Keir states obviously having just spoken to Sailor.

"Go to her bookstore," I tell him.

He instructs the driver, and our car pulls around.

"Why would she be there?" Angelo asks. "It's late."

"She's always there," I grumble.

It isn't long until we come to a stop out the front, and I see the light shining inside.

"Stay in the car," I tell them before I slide out. Keir takes the bottle from my hands as I stumble and push open the door of the bookstore, which is unlocked *yet again*. Does she not care for her own safety?

"*Tesoro*."

"I am *not* your darling," she bites out, her head popping up from behind a bookshelf.

"You are wanted. Why are you still here?" I ask, looking around at the boxes that are everywhere.

"I got a late shipment, and I have to unpack and stock the shelves. The author is coming tomorrow to personally sign them."

"And you think this..." I wave my hands around, "... is more important?" I pick up the book, scrunching my nose at the cover of some shirtless guy. "They said to never judge a book by its cover, but I'm judging. What the hell is that!" I point with a cynical stare at the ridiculousness that's right in front of my eyes.

"Yeah, well, that's what fools do. Maybe you should open it. You might learn a thing or two." She snatches the book from my hand. "You stink, or better yet, you reek of alcohol. Leave before you fuck up my store with that stench that I won't be able to get out before tomorrow morning."

"Keir is sitting in the car waiting for me." Why I

said that I have no idea. Guess I thought he might add some weight to my non-existent argument.

She pauses, looks behind me, then back to me. "You should for sure leave then. I don't want to have to deal with your mafia boss."

"I'm a boss too."

"You are a bitch. Please... get it right."

Goddamn her! I suck in air through my teeth at her words.

"And soon you will be *my bitch*," I snap back.

"If you say so." She smirks at me, then waves her hand toward the door. "Leave and go and be someone else's bitch."

"You are really pissing me off," I warn her, which elicits a zero reaction as she continues to sort through book after book.

"Good. Will it make you leave any faster? Perhaps I should increase my all-around bitchiness."

"No, but it might just make me burn your fucking store to the ground."

Her body and then eyes connect with mine so fast I think her head might fall from her body, but something changes in her eyes. She looks me up and down, and then a condescending smile graces her lips. "That's childish. Grow up. Learn how to handle people calling you names because I can't promise I'll stop any time soon."

The front door opens, and Keir walks into the small, untidy bookstore.

She stays quiet, and I smirk at her uncomfortable stance.

"Adora, here, was just telling me how she doesn't want to go."

Keir looks at me and then at her.

"I have work," she states, motioning to the boxes stacked in front of her.

"Joey will stay and help you."

"Where are you going?" I ask Keir as he spins on his heels and heads straight for the door.

"To collect my wife."

Then he is gone, and she's snickering.

"See? Little bitch, just like I said."

TEN

ADORA

Yes, I know what I said has struck a nerve, but I don't really care. I told him I didn't want to have a bachelorette party, but he didn't listen. I have a job, and that job requires I be here and not drinking or partying with women I hardly know.

"If you call me a little bitch one more time, I'll spank your fucking ass until you're *my* little bitch," he threatens, his voice sounding a bit slurred. When he goes to sit, he almost falls off the chair but manages to catch himself.

Clearly drunk.

"Do you love her?" he asks, confusing me.

"Who?"

"The blonde. Do you love the blonde?"

I'm shaking my head before I realize I am doing it. "I don't know her well enough for that."

"But you haven't ruled out the possibility of falling in love with her?" His eyes stay locked on mine as he leans forward, resting his elbows on his knees while waiting for my response.

When did this conversation turn so deep?

"No, I have not," I reply honestly.

"How do you think that's going to work when you live with me? Which, by the way, *will* be *very* soon."

"She knows about you. It isn't like I'm hiding the fact," I point out, shrugging.

"No one likes to share," he mumbles. "Though I'm not opposed to watching." A dirty smirk touches his lips, and I can't help the puff of laughter that escapes me.

"Is that your kink? Watching?" I ask as I resume putting books away.

"I like to watch."

"I like to fuck," I reply, unsure of why I'm engaging in this conversation. "And I'm not picky about the sex of my partner either." I turn back to look at him. "Are you?"

"Yes, I fuck women, and women only." Like that wasn't already clear as day, but I am goading him.

"Maybe you should try a man. Though, from experience, women fuck so much better." I smirk.

"*I* fuck better. I'd fuck *you* better," he almost mutters.

"If you say so." I try to hide the smile on my lips, but he catches it, and it makes him angry. He begins unbuttoning his jeans then, in one swift movement, he reaches down and pulls out his cock. At the sight, my amusement morphs to shock.

Shock that he did this?

Shock that I'm not completely disgusted?

I'm not sure.

"I'm ready to fuck, are you?" As he says it his cock gets hard, and my eyes widen. He is indeed ready. And, might I add, he has a decent-size cock. Bigger than any I have had before.

My pussy tingles totally without my permission.

Would it hurt if we fucked?

Turning my back to him, I continue to stack the shelves and state, "I'm busy."

He chuckles. Then I hear the shuffling of feet and the slam of a door.

When I turn back around, he's gone.

BECCA IS... beautiful. There's no denying that.

And to top it off, her home is gorgeous. It's a small apartment with only one bedroom, but it's so full of color and life that you instantly feel welcome when you enter. She rang me this morning and asked if I wanted to come over for dinner. And after last night's—whatever you want to call it with Joey—I gladly agreed.

Becca cooked me dinner, and we ate it on her couch while watching *Gilmore Girls*. Now she's lying on my lap while my hand strokes her short hair.

"This situation is going to be messy, isn't it?" she asks, taking her eyes off the television and glancing back at me.

I want to lie to her, to tell her no it won't be and that she has nothing to worry about.

But that would be a lie.

Unless I fly to Italy, grab my sister, and take Becca with me, then attempt to work out some way to hide us all, that's the only way we could possibly not be a part of this upcoming shitshow.

"I hope not," I reply, but it's almost a whisper because I don't believe the words I am saying out loud.

Her eyes search my face, and my heart thumps a bit harder.

"Do you think you'll sleep with him?"

Being not sure how to answer her, I bite my lip at her blunt question, especially after last night, I'm realizing it might be inevitable.

"I want to tell you no, but Joey is attractive. And soon I'll be spending every day with the man. So, I'm not really sure."

She turns away from me and looks back at the television. "We could end it now," she suggests, her tone soft, her eyes still on the screen. "That's the right thing to do, before we both get messy." Becca pulls away and sits up on the couch, reaches for her shirt, and pulls it up and over her head, leaving her in only a bra. Then she stands and drops her skirt to the floor, so she is standing in front of me in only a thin lace G-string.

"I should do it. End this."

She leans forward and cups my cheek. "You should do it. Please do it," she almost begs, then climbs onto my lap. Her legs go around me and her lips find mine.

She tastes different than Joey.

Why on earth am I comparing the two?

She is sweeter, whereas he is sweet and sour at the same time.

Her hand slips under my top until she cups my

breast, then she lifts my shirt and pulls my tit free, breaking our kiss and moving her mouth to my nipple. I moan at her soft lips and the flick of her tongue before I slide my hand between us and touch her through her panties. She's wet, so I push the fabric to the side and slip a finger in while my thumb teases her clit.

Becca starts moving, her hips rocking at my touch, her mouth still on my nipple as her hand slides between us and slips alongside mine. She lightly rubs my clit as she moves her mouth to my other breast.

"Adora."

"Hmm," is all the response I can manage before I pull her head up to meet my eyes, our hands stuck down each other's panties, fucking each other with our fingers. I slam my mouth onto hers, but she kisses me gently. She is always so gentle.

"I don't think I can make this stop. Even knowing where this could lead..."

I move my fingers faster, applying more pressure on her clit. She continues to rub mine, but her movements are all over the place. Then her hand stops, and I know she's nearing the edge. She breaks away from our kiss and leans her head on my shoulder, her hands on my waist, as she rides out the wave enveloping her body while her hips still grind into my hand.

When she comes around my fingers, I stop, and she collapses onto me, her hips still and her breathing heavy.

"And I didn't even use my mouth," I tell her, smiling. She chuckles into my shoulder before she pulls back and climbs down onto the floor and reaches for my shorts. I lift my hips so she can pull them off, along with my panties. She pushes on both of my knees and spreads me.

"No, but I want to." She moves forward and lowers her mouth to my pussy. I somehow slide forward a little more, and my hand grips her short blonde hair as she starts moving her tongue. The first lick sends shivers all over my body, the second pushes me to a place where I am deliriously happy.

Her tongue stays exactly where I need it—on my clit—while her fingers move down and slide into me, pumping in and out with a beautiful rhythm.

My phone starts ringing, and we both ignore it as she continues our pleasure.

And trust me when I say it's pure *pleasure*.

But just as I'm about to come, my mind flashes to someone and something I don't want there—*Joey and his cock.*

She stops when I come.

I grip the couch, and the fingers of her free hand dig into my leg as she lifts her mouth but continues to fuck me with her fingers. She climbs up my body until she is back on my lap, and I open my eyes to see her looking down at me.

"We can continue this in the bedroom." She smirks.

My phone rings again, and she reaches for it without thinking and smiles.

"Hello." I hear a voice on the other side of the line, but don't know who it is. "Yeah, sure, here she is." She hands me the phone.

I glance at the number and don't recognize it. "Hello."

"Hey, Adora. This is Sailor. We've met before. You brought a glorious pair of heels to my house." It's the mafia boss' wife.

And I do remember her—pretty little thing that likes expensive shoes. Lucas bought her a pair as an apology to make up to Keir for something, but he made me deliver them. In exchange, I got a pair too. Because, hello, why the hell would I not be in on that exchange.

"Yes, I remember you," I reply.

Becca leans forward and kisses the top of my breast, her hands grabbing my waist.

"Keir asked that I check in with you on everything for the wedding."

"Check what?" I ask her, my brows furrowing.

"The reception."

"Okay..." I trail off as Becca leans forward and kisses my lips softly before she pulls away and leaves me there to continue my conversation. I hear her refrigerator open and shut before she comes back with a glass in her hand.

"Joey said he was going to ask you for ideas. Did he not do that?"

Becca gets back down on her hands and knees in front of me, pulls a piece of ice from her cup, and puts it in her mouth.

"No."

"Okay, wait a second... I'm going to put you on speaker."

"No, don't," I say, but I don't think she hears me as I hear rustling from the other end.

"I asked Keir if I could help because I can't imagine the stress this will have caused you, and he said to check with you. So, any color preference?"

Becca leans forward and places the ice from her mouth against my clit. I squeal and try to cover my mouth, but she holds me still with her other hand. She slides the ice up to my stomach, and I watch as it melts before she drags it back down again.

"Adora?"

"No, no preference," I squeak out.

"Okay." There is a pause. "And Joey?" she calls out. "Sorry, Joey is here. I'll just check with him."

"I need to go," I say into the phone, my eyes drawn to Becca as she smiles and slips the ice into her mouth and touches my clit with her tongue before she changes it over for the ice.

"Oh my God," I moan out the words so dramatically that I know they will know exactly what's happening.

"What the fuck are you doing?" I hear Joey's voice come over the phone, but I'm not in the right state of mind to deal with him and his shit right now.

"Any color. He can pick. I have to go." I drop the phone just as she slides her tongue right in—where her fingers were earlier— and I scream. Then she fucks me until I see stars.

"Adora."

"Hmm."

"Let's go to bed."

"Can't move."

I hear her chuckle before she picks up my hand

and slides it to her breast. "Adora, I'm not finished yet. Let's go to bed."

"Okay," I say breathily. I'm still palming her breast, and as I stand, I lean forward and bite it. She squeals, and I pull away.

"Do the other," she commands. And I do before I grab both of them and push them together, sucking on each one. "Fuck, are we going to make it to the bedroom?"

"I hope not," I tell her, pushing her back until we're on the floor.

We never make it to the bed or even the bedroom.

ELEVEN

JOEY

"Is she?" Sailor asks.

Chanel chuckles from where she sits, nodding her head. Sailor takes it off speaker and picks the phone up.

"No, put it back." I snatch it from her and place it to my ear.

"So I guess *you* should pick all the wedding things. Or are you happy for me to do it?" Sailor asks me, but I'm too transfixed listening to my future wife get fucked.

Literally.

She moans loudly.

And my dick hardens.

"Joey," Sailor says, but I ignore her. "Are you

both seeing other people? I mean... to each their own, but are you seeing anyone?"

"I am," I snap.

It's a damn lie.

I haven't been with anyone since I saw Adora in the bookstore with a woman between her legs.

"Well, I just wanted to make sure. Are you okay?"

I walk away from her not replying and taking her phone with me as I go. Stepping into the downstairs bathroom, I shut the door and place the phone on speaker again as I sit down on the sink.

Her moans grow louder, and she says something, but it's muffled.

"Adora," I call out, hoping she'll hear me.

But she doesn't by the sounds she's making.

"Fucking hell." My cock strains in my trousers, so I undo them and pull it out. I stroke myself as I listen to her—the way she sounds is enchanting.

I wish it were me who was making her sound like that.

Making her scream *my* fucking name.

My hand pumps harder as her moans seem to grow even louder.

Then louder still.

I can't stop myself, even though I should. I've

only reunited with this little firecracker a week, and she's already under my skin.

Places she should not be.

I dream of fucking her, and I blame her for that.

If my first visual of her wouldn't have been watching her come, would I still want to fuck her this badly? Probably not.

"I need..." Her moans have stopped, and she is huffing now. Her voice is closer to the phone, so I stroke my cock faster, harder.

"Adora," I say her name again, and I don't expect her to answer me back.

"Joey?" I hear the rustling of a phone before she answers, sounding confused. I go to pick the phone up, but I press the video button instead and her face comes into view. She's naked with her breasts on full display, and she's looking right at me.

Her eyes drop to where my hand is located and go wide.

"What are you doing?" It's a hushed whisper only meant for me to hear.

"Adora, come back." I hear the woman who just made her come speak, so Adora turns her head away from me.

"I'll just be a second." Then she walks off, taking

me with her, the phone showing her tits perfectly. Sweet, round, small, perky fucking tits.

"Joey," she hisses, her face coming into view. "What the hell are you doing?"

"What does it look like I'm doing?" I say with a groan, my cock still firmly grasped in my hand.

"It looks like you're giving yourself a hand job while you listen to me fuck my girlfriend."

"Your girlfriend?" I growl.

"Yes, *my girlfriend*. I like her... a lot."

"And what about me?" Her eyes drop to my cock, and I position the phone so she can see clearly.

"I..." She stops talking, her eyes stuck on me for a long moment before she glances away, swallowing roughly. "You need to stop."

"That sounds like a threat," I say, my hand pumping, feeling myself getting closer with every word that leaves her lips, regardless of what they mean.

"Yes, it is."

"What will you give me if I do?" My gaze drifts back to her eyes, and the look in them turning me on even more.

"I-I..." she stutters.

"Not good enough." I cut her off just as I feel myself come.

Adora watches, biting her lip, and when I'm done, I slide my cock into my trousers and lift the phone to my face.

"I could fuck you so hard and good. I want you to remember that when you lie back down next to your *girlfriend*." Then I hang up and walk out of the bathroom.

I find Keir standing there, his hand is outstretched, and I drop the phone into his palm.

"I'll have to burn it now," he says, looking down at it with disgust. "You can explain to my wife why she has to get a new phone." Then he walks off, leaving me standing there staring after him.

"Joey." I turn to Sailor. "What did she say?"

"She said nothing." I smile and step past her. "You need a new phone. I got it wet."

"I have a feeling it wasn't water," Chanel says from not far away, chuckling.

TWELVE

ADORA

Even though I wanted to, I didn't stay the night at Becca's. I ended up going back to my place after that phone call with Joey. That was weird, and hot, and weird. And I may have lied and said she was my girlfriend, though I think he knew that was the case. Even though the evidence says otherwise.

Today is my last day before I walk down the aisle to *him*.

I've spent hours upon hours trying to work out how to get out of it.

But I can't come up with one single thing.

I can't risk my sister's life, even though we aren't close. I would never risk her life for my own. She blames me for our father's death, which she should. I did kill him, after all. And I would do it again.

Every. Single. Time.

That man deserves to be six feet under.

He was vile.

Vindictive.

A true bastard.

I've also avoided going to work so far today, but I have an author signing late this afternoon, and I can't not show up.

I need to hire more staff, but the thought of someone messing up my bookstore hurts me more than I'm willing to admit. I have set it up so it's shelved according to specific romance genres and then color-coded.

It's literally perfect.

My safe haven.

My place to just be me.

When I turn up to unlock the doors, Joey's leaning against the building. I ignore the flutter in my stomach as I look him over. He's dressed nicely today, not in his usual jeans and shirt. He is wearing a blue button-up shirt, sleeves rolled up and show-casing a few tattoos, and his messy curls are slicked back. I hate to say it, but I prefer them when they're messy.

"To what do I owe the pleasure?" I say, striding straight past him to the door.

"You didn't open today."

"No, I didn't."

"Is that something you usually do?"

"No, I've never not opened," I reply over my shoulder. "But then again, I've never had to marry someone I didn't want either."

"Your tits say otherwise." A smirk pulls up at the corners of his mouth as I glance down to see my traitorous nipples high-beaming.

"They have a mind of their own, nothing to do with you."

"Of course, they do. Maybe you should listen to them." He follows me in when I push the door open and switch on the lights.

"That's a hard no. They don't have a brain, but you can rest assured I do."

"Mmm," is all I get in response. I go to the back and get the props and signs for the table, and he leans against the counter, watching me.

"What are you doing?"

"I have to set up. I have an author due in about thirty minutes to sign books. Look, people are already starting to arrive." His head turns to where I nod outside and then he steps closer to me. I'm about to tell him to back off and fuck off, but he speaks before I can.

"What can I do?"

"You want to help?" I ask, my head rearing back, stunned.

"Yes, did I stutter?" he answers as if it's nothing.

"No, but..." I shake my head at him and look out the door at the mounting crowd that is going to be inside shortly, then back to him. "Okay, you can help. Can you please start grabbing the chairs from the back office and bring them out?" He leans down just a little, so his breath tickles my neck.

"Joey."

"Hmm?"

"What are you doing?"

"You have something on your neck," he says. I reach up to touch it, but his hand captures mine. "I can get it." His fingers touch my neck, tickling almost, and I know he is lingering longer than he should.

"What is it?" I ask.

"Just fluff." He steps around me. "But don't worry, I got it." Then he goes to the back room, and my arms are covered in goosebumps from the interaction.

Managing to shake his close proximity off, I get back to work. He brings out every chair and even manages to move one of the shelves for me to make more room in the tight space.

When he's done and the room is set up, the author enters the shop. I smile back at Joey and go over to talk to her. The line outside is long—at least over a hundred people waiting—and I'm so excited to host my first ever book signing. I've been following this author's work for ages, and I admire the way she sucks you into the story from the prologue.

Joey slips out the back as the room becomes more crowded, and as it's finishing up a few hours later, I go into my office to find him sitting at my desk, his legs up, his phone on, and a plate of sushi next to my laptop.

"Eat," he commands. I'm about to tell him no, but he pushes the food my way without looking and stays glued to whatever is on his phone.

"Sailor has been hooked on this show, *Euphoria*. Have you seen it?" he asks, his eyes finally leaving the screen to lock on mine.

I hate that his eyes are so beautiful.

So damn captivating.

He doesn't have to say much to mean much because those eyes say it all.

"No, I don't watch much TV. I read."

He nods as if he gets it. "It's good. You should give it a go."

"I'll think about it." I pick up the first piece of sushi and then say, "Thank you for this."

"You're welcome." He glances at me and goes back to his show.

"Do you think we'll last?" I ask him the question that's been circling in my mind all day every day because really, how is this ever going to work long-term?

He pauses his show, shifts his feet down off my desk, and sits up straight.

"Last?" he asks, leaning forward.

"Yes, us." I wave a finger between us, popping another piece of sushi into my mouth.

"I don't intend to marry another woman in my lifetime."

"That could change. I'm sure your brother didn't want to either, yet he did." I shrug.

"Are you hoping I back out first?"

"Yes," I answer truthfully, and he sighs.

"You know the only way to end the agreement is to be married for ten years or have a baby, so unless you want to jump on this desk, spread your legs, and give me a kid, it's not happening any time soon. Why, do you want to marry your little blonde?"

"I hardly know her." It's a lie, I do know her. Probably better than I have known anyone, and it's only been just over a week. We talk every day for hours. She tells me everything. I know all about from when she went to school to her first kiss with a girl.

She knows a lot about me too, but not everything.

I'm not sure how she would react if she knew I killed my father. That piece of information isn't something you tell someone who isn't in our circle.

I know Joey doesn't care.

He didn't even flinch.

But that's because it's the life he knows.

Death is rarely a shock to people like us. People come and go. You make connections in this world and hope they're strong. That's it. I've tried as much as possible to distance myself from that life, and I thought I had a way out. My first mistake was under-estimating them.

It won't be a mistake I repeat.

"You have feelings for her," he states, his gaze following the movement as I lick soy sauce from my lip before they meet my eyes again.

"I do." I don't even bother lying.

"She's a liability," he argues, then he abruptly stands and walks toward the door. "Your girlfriend is here." And for the first time, I hear the venom in his voice. "I'll see you tomorrow, at our wedding." Then he stalks out, leaving me wondering how tomorrow is going to play out. I push the sushi away, suddenly not so hungry anymore.

"Becca." He growls her name as he passes her, and she enters my office, holding her hands over her chest.

"He doesn't like me very much, does he?" she says, wincing.

"It doesn't matter if he does, it only matters if I do," I reply softly, smiling.

"This is true." She nods. "But he's going to be in your life."

I can't deny that fact.

"I'm moving in with him," I admit. Her mouth drops open, and she looks back over her shoulder, and I think it's so I don't see the look on her face. The hurt, anguish, despair.

"This is a lot."

"It is." I should've told her sooner, but I was trying to pretend it wasn't happening. I can't do that any longer as the time is looming so close now that I need to be totally honest with her. She deserves the truth. She deserves a genuine answer. Becca is a decent woman with, quite frankly, honorable intentions.

"I don't..." She pauses. "I've been trying to work it all out in my head. When I'm with you, I'm happy. You make me happy, Adora."

"You make me happy as well."

She nods as if she understands. "How can this work? I've never had to deal with something like this, and I don't know anyone who has."

"You can walk away, Becca. Today is the day you *should* walk away." I force the words out, pausing and glancing behind her to the author waiting at the door. "It will hurt less if you do it now."

"See, that's the thing... I don't think it will. I think it's going to hurt regardless," she whispers and wipes a stray tear from her eyes before she hurries out of the room.

Did we just end it?

I'm not even sure.

MY EYES FLASH open to knocking on my door. Loud knocking.

I drank a bottle of wine with the intent to pass out and get rid of my thoughts, but it didn't work.

Rubbing my eyes, I walk to the door and pull it open. Three women stand on the other side. And

Troy, who looks incredibly comfortable standing beside them. The thought crossed my mind, *I wonder if he knows they are all connected to the mafia.*

"Gurrrl." His eyes roam me. "You look like utter shit." He pushes his way into my apartment and doesn't stop until he is standing in the middle of the room.

"We've been knocking for ages. Are you okay? We thought you did a runner," Sailor says. I glance down at her shoes and smile. They're the ones I got her from Lucas.

"I drank too much," I mutter as I scan them over one at a time. Chanel, who I know the most, is with Lucas. Piper, who is third-in-command after Joey. And Sailor, who is Keir's wife. And, of course, my best friend, Troy.

"The makeup lady came and left, but lucky for you, Chanel knows how to do it."

Chanel pulls out her bag and sets it on my table. "I've been practicing, and I think I've gotten good at it." She smiles.

"She's great. Look at my face," Sailor says, smiling.

"You need to shower, you stink." Troy grabs me by the shoulders and turns me toward the bathroom.

"We'll be back. Get the wine," he tells the others, smiling and stepping into my bathroom with me. "What on earth? Why do you smell like a brewery?"

"I told you I drank too much."

"Why?" he asks, his hand going to his hip. "And get in that shower."

I start taking off my clothes as he reaches for the faucets and turns them on.

"Becca ended things between us. And, in case you didn't know, I'm getting married today."

"Okay, so which one is worse?"

I step into the shower and let the water wash over my face as I think over his question.

"The breakup. I think I can deal with Joey."

"You don't sound convinced."

"Because I'm not."

"Okay, let's focus on the most important issue at hand... you are about to get married. Where are you going on your honeymoon?"

"Honeymoon?" I squeak, the thought making me more nervous than walking down the aisle.

"Yes, you know, where couples go and fuck the whole time."

"I'm not fucking him." I spit the words out like some bitter-tasting food has been placed in my mouth.

Why didn't I ask him about this sooner?

"Okaaay..." He reaches in, turns off the shower, and hands me a towel. "Get dressed. We have a wedding to get ready for."

"Can I run?" I ask with an innocent smile.

"Ha, you should have run the minute you knew." He closes the door after him as I wrap the towel around myself.

Is running still an option?

THIRTEEN

JOEY

"You think she'll run?" Lucas muses.

"Shut up," I say, doing up my buttons.

"I mean, I would. You're a dick," he says, and I groan.

"Do you really have to be here?" I argue with him.

"Yep, have pity for me."

"Joey," Keir interrupts our bickering. "She's on her way."

On her way.

Almost here.

Fuck.

"Lucas, go and take a seat outside." Lucas heads out at Keir's order, leaving the two of us standing here as I look at myself in the mirror. "Are you nervous?" Keir asks.

"No." I'm not. I like Adora. My option could be a lot worse. My cousin is married to a woman who I'm pretty sure will slit his throat while he sleeps one day soon because she quite simply hates him.

I don't hate Adora, and I hope she doesn't dislike me.

"She will make a good wife."

"You don't know that," I say to him, lifting a brow in question.

He smirks. "No, I don't, but that's what you want to hear, right?"

"No, it's not what I want to hear at all. I want to hear that I am walking down the aisle to a woman I love, just like you had the chance to do."

"You may love her... *one day*."

"I like her, that's it. No love."

"Love takes time." He meets my eyes in the mirror's reflection.

"So does good sex," I reply and pick up a bottle of bourbon, taking a shot.

"Let's go and wait for your bride." Keir holds open the door for me to go first, but I don't want to go.

Cold feet? I don't know.

The woman I am about to marry prefers women.

She will never give me what I want.

What I need.

And I'm not a man to take it.

And the thought of fucking another woman right now doesn't even want to cross my mind.

I love fucking.

I love watching.

She would be a joy to watch.

Of that, I'm sure.

"Joey, she's here," Keir announces.

I follow him out to stand at the end of the aisle. A few of our family are already seated as the back doors open.

She steps in.

Dressed in red.

Her long hair is up, loose curls falling from the back of her ponytail.

And red lips.

Hot.

Red.

Lips.

Just right for ringing my cock!

She doesn't look pleased to be here, so at least we agree on something. But she sure does look beautiful.

"Red," Keir whispers.

He knows it's *my color*.

I wanted her to wear white.

But, of course, she chose something different.

When she reaches me, I offer her my hand, but she refuses, clutching her black roses instead.

"You look beautiful," I tell her, her eyes meeting mine.

"I know," she replies, and a smile plays on my lips.

FOURTEEN

ADORA

I'm not going to lie because the girls did an amazing job. My makeup has stayed the whole time, even after three glasses of champagne, which I hate.

But this day requires champagne or any form of alcohol really.

"I want to go," I tell Joey, who is sitting next to me. We haven't moved from our seats, and I've barely touched the food that has been placed in front of me.

"After we dance," he replies. "Don't you think you've had enough?" He nods to my glass.

"Nowhere near enough," I reply, smiling.

"Adora." I turn to Troy, who is sitting next to me. "Be nice."

I give him an eye roll. "I am," I bite back.

"Let's be honest. You could have had worse. That man is fine with a capital F."

"I can hear you," Joey says from the other side of me.

"And he's also an ass, in case you haven't been able to tell."

"Still hear you." Joey clears his throat, then stands. He turns to face me and gently reaches down and moves my glass to the table before offering me his hand. "Time for our dance."

"I don't want to," I argue with him.

"Too bad. Now get up."

"Yeoowww," Troy says.

I give Joey my hand, and he helps me to stand before guiding me to the dance floor. Everyone starts clapping, and I avoid making eye contact with anyone around us.

"Didn't take you for the shy type," Joey remarks as we get to the dance floor. He pulls me into him so our bodies are touching and puts his hands on my waist.

I feel it.

I feel him.

Everywhere.

His touch is warm and inviting.

I hate that.

Hate that my body likes it.

That it likes *him*.

It's a deceiving little bitch.

"I'm not shy." Our bodies are locked tight, my hands resting on his shoulders as the song plays. I can't even tell you what song it is. All I can hear is the rhythm of my own heart beating. It's the alcohol. That must be the reason he's having an effect on me.

"You'll be staying with me tonight," he states, making my feet halt where they are. He notices before he steps on my foot and looks down at me. "You knew this was going to happen."

"I like my place."

"Sell it."

"I don't want to sell it." I try to pull back, but his grip doesn't waiver.

"You can sell it and put that money into your bookstore and hire someone," he suggests. I hear the logic in his words, even his soft delivery, but I don't want to reason with him because I don't want him to be right.

"I don't want to share a bed with you."

He says nothing, but I hear him take a deep breath.

"Why are you so calm through all this? This is a fucked-up situation." He pulls back this time. His hand catches my wrist, and he tugs me, angrily, but his grasp is still gentle. I follow him until we get to a back room, and he slams the door shut behind us.

He turns to face me, then starts pacing back and forth. Stopping, he looks at me quickly, his eyes wild, then he resumes his pacing.

"Is this a panic attack?" I ask him, confused by what is going on.

Someone knocks on the door.

"Fuck off," he growls.

We hear footsteps before he turns and faces me again.

"What?" I ask him.

"Is this what I want?" He scoffs and waves his hand up and down my body. "A fucking woman who prefers pussy over cock." He shakes his head. "Is this what I want? A woman who is annoying at every fucking turn." He takes a breath, and I'm about to speak, but he holds up his hand. "You are *not* what I want. I would prefer to marry who I want, who I *love*, but because of the stupid fucked-up life I am living, I get *you*." He snarls the word then continues, "*You...* you are the last thing I want." Then he turns and storms out, leaving me standing there by myself, feeling sick to my stomach.

I didn't expect that from him. Not that I thought he was nice, but he's been so easy-going about this.

"Adora." Troy opens the door and steps in, then closes it behind him. "You really pissed him off. What did you do?"

I shrug my shoulders.

"Seems we both don't want this," I say, sighing.

"Yeah, well, that much is obvious. He's been tense all night while you sat there drinking yourself to sleep." I manage a tight smile. "Come on, you need to make amends. At least find some common ground."

"He wants to share a bed."

"Is that such a bad thing? You have seen him, right?" He waves his hand in front of my face, and I push it away. "Just making sure you ain't blind or anything."

"I have eyes. I can see he's good-looking."

"Okay, just checking. He didn't go back into the wedding reception area. Instead, he went out back." Troy opens the door and nods for me to follow him. I pick up the front of my dress and make my way down the hall. We get to a back door, and Troy pulls it open. Cold wind assaults my body, and I shiver. I see Joey straightaway, a cigarette to his lips and a dog at his side. *Why on earth is a dog there?*

He glances back at us and leans down to pet the dog.

"Maybe if you're a good girl, he'll pet you too, if you know what I mean." Troy winks at my scowl before he turns and goes back inside.

"What do you want, Adora?" The dog starts growling, and Joey pets it some more. "Good boy."

"So, we both hate the situation."

"You sure as shit ain't making it easy..." He scratches the dog behind the ear, then stands, putting the cigarette to his lips and taking a draw.

"I hate smokers," I say as a trail of smoke drifts over me.

"I don't give two shits." He smirks, and it's a big *fuck-you* smirk.

"You can fuck who you want, we've established this," I remind him, albeit hesitantly.

"I believe in marriage," he replies, surprising me. "Maybe not the conventional type, but I do."

"Okaaay..." And here I thought this couldn't get any more confusing.

"You want to fuck your little blonde. I heard how she made you come. Have you thought for just a second I could do the same thing?"

I haven't, have I?

I've been with a few men, and some were okay

lovers. But none knew how to please a woman correctly, the way another woman can with her mouth. Not that they can't, it just seems to take them a shitload longer.

We stand there in silence while he continues to pet the dog, unsure of what to say to each other. He glances my way, a puff of smoke leaving his lips that I remember kissing. And I can see the appeal. I mean, it's not just because I've drunk several glasses of champagne. Joey is a good-looking man.

"Okay, let's fuck, then." I can't believe those words just left my mouth.

I don't think he can either because his hand leaves the dog, and he stands tall. He shakes his head and drops his cigarette, putting it out with his boot.

"You're drunk. We aren't having this conversation. You need to go to bed. And I need bourbon... a lot of it." He goes to walk past me, but my hand shoots out and stops him.

"Will you not even kiss me?" The question leaves my lips as more of a plea. And I instantly hate it. Why am I even stopping him? Why not just let him leave and get away with sleeping in my own bed for one more night?

We didn't kiss after our vows. I turned my head at the last minute, and his lips brushed the side of my mouth. He didn't make a sound, just kissed me, then pulled away.

"I will kiss you." He pauses, leaning closer so he's only a hair's breadth away. "When you actually want it." Then he moves around me and walks to the door, pulls it open, and looks back. "You can go where you want, I'm going out. Happy fucking wedding day."

Once he disappears, I stand there in my red dress, alone, the dog having run away, and the alcohol I drank earlier seems to have left my system like a traitor.

This is what I wanted, right? For him to *not* want me. I'm getting my way. So why is there a dull ache at the thought of him not wanting me?

"So, it seems we have to talk." I spin at the sound of Keir's voice as he shuts the door behind him.

My hands squeeze shut as I wait for him to speak.

Is he out here to kill me?

He is known to take a life as easy as he takes one breath.

"Joey left." I nod solemnly, already knowing this. "He is a good man, and he will follow orders. It's one of the reasons he is my second-in-command. Not because he is my brother, but because he is loyal. Extremely loyal..." He pauses, then steps closer to me, and my heart stutters. "You may not agree with our ways, and I may not even agree with them much of the time, but he does. He trusts in the old ways, and he expects this marriage to work. So why are you fighting him at every turn? Is it because you want that woman?"

I'm stunned.

I don't know what to say.

"No, I don't know him."

"Have you even given him a chance?" he asks. "Or are you just fighting everything to be stubborn? Because if there is one of us who would make a great husband and be loyal, it's Joey. So either get your shit together or... I'll kill you. It's that simple." When he pulls the door open to go back inside, Sailor is standing there. She offers me a small wave and reaches for her husband.

"Hey, Adora, we're gonna head home. You look beautiful." I wave at her.

Keir turns back to look at me. "You understand what I said?" he asks, and I'm nodding before I can get myself to speak. "Yes."

He nods once, and they walk off.

I wait a few minutes before I go inside. And when I do, Becca is standing there, Troy next to her. He seems uneasy.

"You came," I say, surprised, a flicker of happiness shining through me. But it's quickly wiped away as Keir looks back before they disappear around the corner, and I know without him saying anything, it's a warning. He may be known as heartless, but he clearly wants good things for his brother.

"I wasn't sure if I should. I couldn't watch the ceremony." She pulls her hands in tight to herself. I look to Troy to see him side-eyeing me.

"I have to find him. I have to find a way to make this work."

"I think you should," Troy agrees, and Becca stares down at the floor. I step up closer to her and pull her arm free from her chest. Gripping it, I give it a squeeze.

"I do wish I met you at a different time, different place..." I smile. It's soft and sad. "But, Becca, you are amazing. Someone is going to love every piece of you. You will get to have every part of someone soon. It's just not going to be me. I have to give pieces to him, even if I don't want to. I have to try at least. You get it, right?"

"I'm not going to lie and say I do because I don't. This whole world..." she waves her hands around, "... is so out of the realm I live in."

"I grew up in it, tried to escape it once, and it

brought me right back. And I think no matter what, that's what it's going to do until the day I die." She nods, tears pooling in her pretty eyes, before silently walking away. I go to follow her, but Troy reaches for my arm, stopping me.

"Don't chase her, Adora. She isn't the one you just married."

Don't I know that.

The 'Nice' Brother

It seems the bride has an eye for the ladies and not
just her husband.
Do you think this new marriage will work?
Or will it end in destruction?

FIFTEEN

JOEY

There's no way I planned to come here. It's just kind of where I ended up.

I'm wearing a red wristband, and Jake is sitting next to me, counting money.

"Didn't think I'd see you in here," he says and looks around before going back to his wad of hundred-dollar bills. He is the only one without a wristband on—everyone knows who he is.

"I got married."

Jake stops counting, and surprise flashes in his eyes as he looks at me.

"Shit, congrats. When?"

I glance at my watch. "A few hours ago."

"Fuck, why are you here, then?"

"Because it seems my wife is a cunt." I smile nicely.

"Aren't they all?" He chuckles. "Remind me to never get married." His hand lifts, and he pushes his long hair back out of his face.

A girl approaches him and leans on the counter—she's dressed in red lace lingerie and she's beautiful. "I want to go home," she whines, and Jake laughs at her.

"You say that every time you work and never go," he replies.

"I want to live a rich-girl life, Jakey. Can't you be my sugar daddy and support my obnoxious habits?"

"And what habits are those?" he asks, playing into whatever game it is they have.

"Oh, you know... designer bags, designer heels, never cooking again, having a maid and a chef. You name it, I want it."

"Petra, you have all those things. I pay you very well, so you can afford them."

She flicks her hair over her shoulder and turns to me. "I could make you a happy man tonight."

This isn't your average sex club. This is one where when you enter, you wear wristbands to show your willingness. Some people come alone, but some come with their significant other. Or, you have the few like Petra, who are paid to walk around and, if need be, provide those desires of other people. She has been working with Jake for as long as we've been coming here, but we usually don't speak. She is working or I come in here to blow off steam.

In the form of a bed.

We all have our kinks.

"I'm sure you could, but I don't supply my woman with all those things."

"Well, damn, why did I marry you?" We all turn to the voice behind us, but I know who it is before I see her. Adora stands there in her wedding dress, her hair now down, and her phone in her hand.

"Wow! I want a dress like that, Jake. Please, can I have a dress like that?"

"Petra, it's time you go back to work." Jake waves her off, but before she leaves, she leans into Adora. "If he doesn't give you those things, I would suggest divorce." She walks off, and Adora manages a smile. Her eyes flick to Jake, then they scan the room. I notice she has on a yellow wristband. Green means you are up for anything, red is no touching, and yellow is basically a maybe.

Jake stays quiet as he sits there counting his money, and I watch her. Her red lips—those lips that I want to staple shut and kiss at the same time—are slightly parted, and her shiny chocolate-colored hair tumbles messily over her shoulders.

"I've never been to a place like this," she states and looks back at me. "Do you come here often?" Jake barks out a laugh, and her eyes dart to him, then back to me. "You do." She answers her own question. "You either like to watch or enjoy fucking a lot."

My response is to say nothing.

She licks her red lips before she glances at the band on my wrist. "You like to watch, right?"

"I'm going to leave." Jake stands and turns to face Adora. He offers his hand. "It is a pleasure meeting you. Never thought this man would get married, yet... here we are."

"Yes, here we are," I say, smiling, my eyes never leaving her.

"Adora. Nice to meet you." She shakes his hand. "I'm Jake, and you are welcome here anytime."

Turning back to the bar, I tap it for the bartender to bring me another drink.

"I'll have what he's having." The bartender nods before he walks off. "Let me guess, you're trying to work out all the ways to kill me?" She reaches for my glass and takes a sip before placing it back on the bar.

"My toaster is waterproof, so that's out of the question," I tell her. She throws her head back and laughs. The skin of her long neck, bare and sun-kissed, glows under the fluorescent light. "Though I'm sure I could find something. What are you allergic to?" The bartender picks that moment to deliver her drink, and she wipes the tears from her eyes from her laughter and picks it up.

"I would say men..."

"Ha! Guess we're both shit out of luck."

"Guess we are." She reaches over and taps the band I'm wearing. "You like to watch. Is that what you'd like?"

"What?"

"As a wedding present. Would you like to watch me?"

"Watch you?" I ask because I don't believe the words leaving her mouth.

"Yes. Would you like to go to one of those beds and watch me fuck myself in this wedding dress?"

I mean, I'm only human...

SIXTEEN

ADORA

I've pleasured myself before. Many times.

Have I ever had someone watch?

No.

Do I want him to watch?

Possibly.

I know Joey is attractive.

I'm not blind.

I can see that out of all the men available, he is probably the best choice for me.

Does that mean I want to be married?

No.

Again, not my choice.

But I need to try, even if it's not something I would have chosen for myself.

He doesn't seem all that shocked by my question, just more caught off guard.

I like sex. Despite my past, I do.

"Joey, I need words." The music is loud all around us and in some ways distracting.

"Why would you offer that?"

Who the hell asks that? A monk.

"Why?" I narrow my eyes. "Why?" I say again.

"Yes, Adora. Why?"

"Because I need to give a little, and this is me giving a little."

A soft smirk touches his lips. "I have a feeling you never give." He's correct. I give when I receive. Never the other way around. I've been taken my whole life, so when I am in control, I take.

"Yes or no, Joey? You want to watch me hike up this very expensive wedding dress or not?"

He stands and nods his head. "Yes."

"Lead the way," I say, waving.

As he steps past me, he reaches for my wrist and clasps his hand around it. He's strong, and if he applied more pressure, I have a feeling he would hurt my wrist badly. We walk past a few people, most in the midst of fucking or touching. One girl locks eyes with me and gives me a small wave, but I look away and continue following Joey. We go down a hallway, and when we get to the end, he opens a door and holds it for me.

I'm confused.

He sees it written on my face.

"Get in the room, Adora."

His demand makes me want to say "No, get fucked." But I listen, and after I enter the softly lit room, the door shuts behind me with Joey on the other side of it.

Why did he leave me in here alone?

I don't get it.

What is going on?

The room is void of furniture except for a bed situated behind me.

"Adora." I glance at the mirror in front of me and realize it could be a two-way mirror. "Touch yourself."

"Can you see me?" I ask.

"Yes, now do it."

"So demanding," I tease, turning around and giving him my back. Reaching behind me I start to slowly undo the zipper until it gets to my ass. The dress falls into a heap onto the floor at my feet. I step out of it, still in my heels, and head for the bed climbing on. I have no panties or bra on, so the only thing I'm wearing is my heels.

My hands glide across the bed, my ass now in full view, as I spread my legs a little farther. Looking over my shoulder to where I know he is watching from, I smile. "You might want to tell me where?" I give my ass a little shake, and I wonder what expression is written all over his face right now.

"You know what you're doing, so do it." His voice booms through the room.

"Okay." I lay my chest fully on the bed, my hips still up with my ass in the air, and I snake my arm down my center. Reaching between my legs, I touch my pussy, gliding my fingers through the folds.

"Check the drawer." I pull my hand back and stand, walk over to the drawer, and pull it open to find a purple vibrator. Now, this I know how to use. I can usually make myself come faster with one of these than any man could make me. Going up to the mirror, I turn the vibrator on and lift it to my breast, circling my nipples. I slowly slide it down my body until it just starts to tease my clit.

I pull it away when I feel the pleasure building.

With my other hand, I put a finger into my mouth, soaking it before I move it to my clit.

I'm horny.

And I want the release.

Now.

Putting the purple toy to my clit, the vibrations send shockwaves straight through me, but I manage to pull it away before it can make me come. I step back, knowing I'll need to sit for this, so I sit my ass back on the bed. I prop my feet on the edge, legs open, heels digging into the mattress, giving a perfect view to whoever is on the other side of that wall.

"I'm going to come now," I tell him, and he doesn't respond.

Putting the purple pussy-eating machine to my clit, I let it do its job.

And believe me, it does not take long.

I start counting in my head, thinking it will help. Slow me down. But by the time I reach twelve, the pleasure is there, ready for me to fall over into the abyss. My head drops back, my mouth opens, and unintelligible words fly from my mouth.

I don't even know if they're in English.

I pay no attention as I move the purple toy lower, push it inside me, and pull it back out to my clit.

It's a game of cat and mouse between my pussy and my clit.

"Stop!" His voice sounds closer, but I can't seem to lift my head to look in his direction. *Is Joey in the room now?* I don't really care.

"Adora." The word is almost a growl.

I almost pause what I'm doing, but my mind thinks better of it and tells me to not stop, to keep on going because I'm *almost* there. That sweet spot that I crave is *almost* mine.

"Fucking hell." I find him then, those icy blue eyes locked straight on me. And if I didn't know better, I would say he's mad, but as my eyes betray me and glance down, I see his trousers are tight, he's biting his bottom lip, and his hands are clenched to his sides. He's holding something back, but I don't give two shits right now.

I hear the scream as it's ripped from my throat— the scream that I caused, the one that he's enjoying watching me cause.

My legs collapse to one side, and I feel one of my shoes fall off the bed. The vibrator drops in between my legs, my hands fall limply to either side of me. My eyes are glued to the ceiling as the shockwaves run through me over and over again.

"Happy fucking wedding day," I mumble to him, but when I sit up, I see his backside as he walks out the door.

Well, okay then.

Rising to my feet, I pull the big dress back on and zip it up before I walk out the door with a huff.

Joey is nowhere to be seen.

"Miss." My eyes find the guy Joey was talking to. "Or should I say Mrs?" he asks.

"Adora," I remind him and offer him my hand. He looks at it but doesn't touch it, so I let it drop to my side and wipe it on my dress.

"Joey left you this." He hands me a key and heads back to the bar.

"What's it for?"

The man stops and glances over his shoulder. "It looks like a house key," he replies simply, then walks off.

I'm meant to move in with him.

Live with him.

Does that start tonight?

He said as much, right?

I don't know the rules. And, frankly, I don't even want to be here.

How could he just leave me after that? Clearly, he enjoyed the show I put on for him, I saw the evidence in his trousers.

But then he simply left? Why?

I grab my purse from the coat check and pull out my phone.

I message him. I need to know why he walked out like that.

Where are you?

I WAIT, but it isn't until I'm in the Uber that I see the dots indicating he's writing back to me.

And now I'm pissed.

So mad.

I gave up something good for him. I felt good with Becca, and it's been an extremely long time since someone has made me feel that happy. Maybe it was stupid of me to end things with Becca.

Dammit! I should have just run away with her.

Busy.

How dare you just leave me there on the bed. I know you enjoyed it.

I ADD a few angry face emojis and throw my phone into my bag. When the Uber pulls up to my place, I get out and hear the phone ringing. I ignore it, not even caring who it could be, and head inside.

**It wasn't me you were thinking about
when you touched yourself.**

I READ his message and guilt slams into me. *He's right.*

It wasn't him I thought about.

SEVENTEEN

JOEY

I wore pink socks, but do you think she even noticed? No.

The funny part is that she acts like I wanted to marry her, that it was my choice. I didn't want to fucking marry her. I'd rather never fucking marry a single soul in my fucking life than to have married *her*.

I like women—women to fuck, women to kiss.

Beyond that, why the fuck do I need a woman when I can do everything else my fucking self. She gets on my last nerve, and she clearly doesn't want to be around me. And it wasn't me she was thinking about when she held her hands to her pussy.

Does she even like men?

She wants *her,* and I'm just in the way.

If I could change our situation, I would in a heartbeat. I find her attractive, fuckable. There is no fucking point in lying about that. But why would I choose to be with someone who doesn't want to be with me? I can have my choice of women, and she isn't even someone I would pick willingly, normally. That's the most fucked-up part about this whole situation, the woman isn't even my type. And yet, when she dropped her dress and lay on that bed, I looked through the one-way mirror and wanted her.

I wanted my name to leave those fucking lips as she got off, but when I walked into that room it wasn't my name she screamed. That's what made me turn and walk the fuck out of there. She had called out *hers*.

"What are you doing here?" I don't turn around and don't even fucking bother answering. *What's the point?* "Joey." I put the drink to my lips and drain the last of the bottle before smashing it as hard as I can. The glass is all over my hands, and it's all over the fucking floor. I stand and turn around to face my brother. He's still dressed in the same outfit from *my... fucking... wedding*. I want to laugh at how ironic it is, and I'm pretty sure a small chuckle does slip from my lips.

"Do you ever think how fucking ironic it is that

you avoided this fucking bullshit of arranged marriages, and I'm the one who's stuck in one? It's always the fucking way, isn't it?"

Keir doesn't say a word at first, he simply looks at me. His silence is usually not a good sign, but right now, I don't give two shits. I'm the one who has to live in the situation while he gets to go to bed every fucking night with the woman *he chose*, a woman who wants *him*, not to a motherfucking whore who fucked someone else the night we saw each other again for the first time.

"Joey, take a fucking breath and go and get some fucking sleep."

Now I laugh, and even to my ears it sounds manic. Pushing straight by him, my shoulder knocking his, I head to the kitchen. Opening the cabinets, I grab another fucking bottle. He wants me to leave? Well, tough shit for fucking him! He can't have everything he wants, can he? Oh, for fuck's sake, that's right, he can and he has.

"If you weren't my brother..." I wave my hand in the air, "... and my fucking boss, I'd shoot you right between the *fucking* eyes." I make a fake gun and point it at him before I reach for the bottle. He's quick, though, not having drunk as much as me, snatching it from my hand. The minute he does, I grab the closest knife and put it to his neck. He doesn't even flinch, but why would he? I'm his fucking brother, but he should know better because we've killed for less in this family. Fuck, we killed my cousin for disobeying a simple order.

"I suggest you put that knife down," he says it in a calm voice. I am in his house after all.

"Kill her," I tell him. "Kill her, or I fucking will."

"You'll do no such fucking thing. Did she kill your fucking imaginary puppy? Stop being such a child and go home to your fucking wife." He releases himself from my hold and walks off, the knife dropping down to my side as I watch him leave.

"Fuck you, you fucking cunt." He turns and quickly strides back to me, where he puts his hands around my throat. "Do it! Fucking do it! I fucking dare you to do it. I don't fucking care if I live."

His hands drop as he shakes his head. "Sleep it off, Joey. Don't make me come back down here while my wife and children are sleeping. I can assure you that you won't like that side of me. Drink until you pass out, I don't fucking care. But tomorrow when I wake up, you better *not* be here." He leaves, and I reach for the closest bottle of anything and down the entire thing.

Happy fucking wedding day to me.

EIGHTEEN

ADORA

He wasn't there when I arrived last night. But did I really expect him to be? I've pissed him off, and out of the lot of them, he seems like the calmest.

I ended up passing out on his couch, curled up in my wedding dress. And that's where I am when the door flings open this morning and he walks in, still dressed in his suit and looking worse for wear. His eyes find me and drag them down over my body, slow and deliberate. I'm about to smile until a sour expression touches his lips.

Joey shakes his head and continues past me without saying a word.

I thought when I willingly gave him something of me last night, I was trying, but he doesn't seem to appreciate the gesture and that just makes me mad.

How fucking cold and ruthless does someone have to be to not want their wife as she lies on a bed, and he watches her come.

Fuck this.

Hiking my dress up, I get off the couch and stalk up the stairs to his bedroom—the room I'm meant to share with him. When I enter, I hear the shower running in the en suite, and I almost stop myself from barging in. Crunching my dress in one hand, I push the bathroom door open with the other. Steam fogs up the mirror and the glass of the shower door, but I can just make out his form. He has his head leaned against the tiles, body under the spray, and he's breathing heavily.

Is he angry?

Frustrated?

I don't know him well enough to tell, but I know he isn't pleased.

"It's rude to leave your wife after she comes, wouldn't you say?"

He doesn't even react to the sound of my voice, and at first, I think he might be asleep. I've never met someone who can stand and sleep at the same time, but his breathing picks up, getting heavier.

"Joey."

"What."

I try not to ogle him, but, I mean, his ass is right there. However, we need to talk, so I try to keep my eyes above his waist.

I throw my hands up in the air, but he doesn't see me. "Did you not hear a word I just said?"

"The other room is yours. I suggest you go to it and leave me the fuck alone." Again, his voice is rough, but he doesn't turn around to face me as he speaks.

"I don't want to be here anymore than you do, Joey, so maybe you should change your fucking attitude." Just before I turn to leave, he finally faces me, and I stop dead. He has a perfect body. He's chiseled in places I didn't even know a man could be chiseled. His sides look like they have abs—*how is that even possible?* And his six-pack sits just above a perfect V that leads to a beautiful cock. I've seen my fair share of cocks, and his is definitely beautiful. My eyes drag along his skin, taking in several random tattoos over his legs and a few on his hands. When my gaze returns to his face, he's watching me.

Those icy blue eyes are locked on me, but not in a friendly way. He's staring at me as if I'm the worst person to have ever graced this earth, and if his eyes could kill me, they would. This is the part when I probably should back away and give him space, but no one ever claimed I was a smart girl. I'm fucking mad. I'm mad that he thinks he can be angry at me for a situation I don't even want to be in.

"Should I change my fucking attitude?"

He throws his head back and laughs and then it stops as fast as it began. "Never. I think you should be a good little slut and come in here and suck my fucking cock." He pauses to smirk, but he isn't finished yet. "Or just be a good fucking little wife... either or will do."

"How fucking dare you." My feet are moving before I can even stop myself, and now I'm standing in the shower, the front of my dress getting soaked. We're toe to toe now, and I can only imagine his smirk is meant to communicate a thought of *what the fuck are you gonna do about it?*

"What are you going to do about it, darling?"

Huh, maybe I can read him better than I thought?

My blood is absolutely boiling. Who does he think he is? Oh, that's right, my damn husband. Now that's a laugh.

"Darling?" I give him my best eye roll and stick my finger in his face. "I'm going to 'darling' you six feet under the fucking ground. How about that, *darling*?"

I take a small step back, and my eyes disobey me,

glancing down at his cock again. It's not hard to miss, it is right there after all.

"I heard if you take a picture, it'll last longer." I don't give him the satisfaction of looking away from his cock. A part of me wonders what it would be like if that thing comes at me. The other part, though, it wants to cut it off.

"I'm just trying to work out if this is considered small or average." We both know I'm lying. He isn't considered either, but his cock twitches at my words, and his voice follows soon after.

"Why don't you wrap your lips around it, *darling,* and we can test your theory for ourselves."

"Your cock is lucky to be in the same vicinity as me." I move to walk away, but he catches my forearm and turns me back to face him.

"I've been around you. I've seen the face you make when you come, don't forget that. And let's get one thing straight, I'm more and a better man than you could ever get. So why don't you run along and chase that pussy that you're so dying have. Because I don't fucking want you."

"I was willing to try, you know." I wave my hand between us. "But you're all kinds of fucked-up. I fucking tried, and this is what I get back."

He laughs at me again, and my muscles tense with frustration.

"That's cute. That's real, *real* cute that you think you tried. You may have thought you were trying when I stepped into that room with you." He steps closer to me now, so close I can feel his hot breath on my face as he speaks. "But it wasn't my name that left those lips when you came, was it?"

Shit. What? I didn't even realize I said what he thinks I said. I wonder if it's because the last person to make me come was *her*, so it was *her* on my mind. I can see why he's pissed off, but he has to get over it. He can't make this a thing—a one-word slip-up and everything is ruined. I have to be in this relationship as much as he does, so the least he can do is give me some grace when I was falling for someone else, and I stopped that to be with him.

"I can see the wheels spinning in your head. Don't even think for a second you can somehow turn this around on me." He starts to spin away from me, and I do the stupidest thing I can think of doing. I mean, I don't even know why it entered my head. It's the sleep deprivation, that's what I'm going to put it down as. That has to be the reason why my hand reaches out and clutches his cock because there's literally no other reason I can think of as to why I would do something like that. I mean, apart from the fact that it's so pretty, but I'm *never* telling him that.

My eyes shoot up to his as my hand remains wrapped around him. His eyes, that were full of hatred a moment ago, are now full of amusement and perhaps a little bit of shock because here I am, his wife who has never even touched him before, now standing in front of him in a wedding dress in his shower and holding his cock. I mean, when you think about it, it sounds like something a married couple would do, but we aren't your average married couple.

"At least give it a kiss while you're strangling it, darling." My hand drops from him and goes back to bunching my dress up at my side. It would be really wise to walk out of this room right now and not think about what I just did, but I like a bit of a challenge, and Joey will not defeat me.

"You're drunk," I state, realizing I can smell the whiskey on his breath. Had he been drinking all night? I mean, it's morning now. I slept on the couch and heard him come in, but he didn't say a word to me as he walked past and kept going. *What was he doing up all night after he left me stranded in a sex club?*

"Ding, ding, ding. And the prize for the smartest girl in the room goes to you. How would you like your prize, orally, with my fingers, or with my cock?" He puts his back toward me, his smooth ass now on display right in front of me.

And with that, I'm not about to leave without completing this game, so I turn around and take just one step out of the shower, unzip my dress, let it drop to the floor, then step back into the shower, reaching past him toward the soap. He's turned his head ever so slightly and his eyes scan down my body, assessing me the same way my eyes assessed him. I should shy away—I mean, he's told me before that I'm too skinny and I'm not his type—but I don't because the anger is stronger than the shame.

"Did you want to play, darling?" he taunts.

I start washing myself and look up at him. "Play with you? Now that's a laugh and a half. Who the fuck would want to play with you, *darling*?"

Don't look at his cock!

Don't you dare look at his cock!

Not wanting to give him the impression that this is what I want because is this really what I want? I think that's the problem. I was figuring out what I wanted and what I needed, then everything just got piled on top, confusing me even more.

With Becca, I was happy, but a small part of me thought this could be a life for me. What a joke that was because life isn't ever that easy. My life has never been, and it never will be.

"I've played nice with you. I've been on my best behavior, even after you fucked someone else," he states. I go to tell him that I was fucking her before I even met him and he knew it, but he holds a finger to my lips, ultimately shutting me up before he continues, "I like to consider myself a fair, nice man, even sensible, but when I'm fucking pushed…" He takes a deep centering breath. "You have pushed me to the edge, not even willing to try. And when you were there, making your sorry attempt, you reverted to someone else. This marriage is going to be the fucking death of me if I don't kill you first." His curly hair hangs on his face and his full lips are pressed thin as he glares at me. "Now, I'm going to bed, *darling*. Do *not* fucking wake me."

I don't say a word as he turns and grabs a towel.

My eyes drop to his ass as he exits the bathroom, not even stopping to dry himself. I hear a door slam shut, and I wonder *how the fuck can I get out of this*.

NINETEEN
JOEY

Joey

My head is fucking pounding. I roll over, and the first thing I see is the ring on my finger. Scrubbing my hands down my face, I think to myself, *what the fuck?* That's a normal reaction to have after you marry someone you don't want to marry, right? I mean, let's be honest, who in this fucking day and age does arranged marriages? Oh, that's right, my ridiculous family. I understand when it's for religion, but this little move Keir made was simply for power. My family is all about the power.

"You're awake." The ringing in my ears fucking

hurts. I pull my hands away from my face and wince when I open my eyes and see Adora standing there, looking happy as can be, dressed in a pair of short cut-off jeans, a white singlet, her hair dead straight, and an unnecessary smile on her face.

When I don't reply, her smile grows even wider. "Your mother is here."

"Oh..."

"Yes, and she wants to see the happy couple. Now, I know fuck all about mothers because mine ran away the minute she could and left me with daddy dearest, but yours seems..." She holds up an okay sign with her fingers. "I don't mind pissing you off, Joey. That, I can deal with. But your mother? Nope! No way. She is currently downstairs cooking us lunch." She glances at her watch. "Because, you know, you've been sleeping for the last six hours."

I close my eyes at her words.

Six hours? Is that all?

Fuck, I need at least ten more.

"Now, get the fuck up and deal with your mother with me because, unlike you, I need to make a good impression on her." With that, she turns and walks out the door.

My mother is a hard yet amazing woman. Along with my brother, she is one of the only people in this world who I don't want to disappoint. She's had her fair share of fucked-up life being married to my father. We saw it growing up, and I vowed to never be the man he was. He was a mafia boss, and he was in an arranged marriage with my mother, just like I am with Adora, but he treated her like utter shit. He even went so far as to fake his own death to run away with the woman he was sleeping with behind my mother's back.

And then, to add to the shitty things he'd done, he came back because he wasn't happy with how Keir was running things. He said Keir should've stuck to his arranged marriage to a fucking lunatic. Kier ended up having to kill our father, which wasn't easy for him, but it wasn't exactly hard either. Keir has only loved two women in his life—the one he's married to and the one who is downstairs currently cooking me lunch. I've only loved one. And I'm not sure I can love the other woman in my house right now. I don't think I even fucking want to.

Getting out of bed, I go straight for the drawers and pull on a pair of shorts and a shirt before going down the stairs to where I can hear my mother's voice.

My mother didn't approve of Keir's choice in wife at first, but now they are extremely close. And I expect the same thing from her regarding Adora and me. But when I reach the bottom of the staircase, I hear my mother's laughter. When I round the corner, I see flour all over the kitchen counter and her rolling out dough. Adora sits on the other side and watches, holding a glass of wine in one hand, a smile strapped to her face as my mother tells her a story.

As soon as I enter, my mother raises her head, her eyes light up, and her smile brightens. "Oh, my baby's awake."

Adora turns around and doesn't offer me a smile, merely glares at me before turning back to face my mother.

"I was just telling Adora about how you were when you got your first girlfriend in high school and how your brother ran her off because you were destined to marry someone else." Keir and I have always been close. Not your normal, average brotherly close, but more on the side of we don't lie to each other, and we are protective, even when we shouldn't be.

I grew up in a household where nothing revolved around me. Everything was done in preparation for my brother to step up and take over from my father. I was naïve and young and thought I could get away with everything because I didn't have to worry about *this life.* This life that I have been handed and will always be a part of. But when Kier took over, he brought me with him, made me his second-in-command. It wasn't by force. I willingly went because that's what family does.

My brother was trained to kill at a young age, and the first time I ever took someone's life was when I was seventeen, and they had a gun to my brother's head. I had no other choice. And ever since then, I haven't been able to back away. Seventeen is considered late in my world to get your first kill, but I'm in this life now, and there is no getting away from it.

"I lost my virginity to her," I share. Adora almost spits her wine out, and my mother looks at me, shocked.

"Joey, I don't think that's something that you should announce so proudly, do you?" my mother scolds.

All I give her is a shrug.

"Anyway, I'm making pizzas for you and Adora. We have family coming over tonight to congratulate you and bring gifts, so do you think you can dress?" my mother says, waving her hand at what I'm wearing. Adora laughs again over her wine glass.

"And what about what she's wearing? Do you think that's acceptable?" Adora licks her lips, trying to hide a smirk, while my mother's mouth hangs open in shock. "I would say it's a bit trashy, wouldn't you?"

"That's it." My mother holds up her finger, and I know I've made her mad, but the smirk still sitting on Adora's lips makes me even madder. "March right up those stairs and don't come back down until you have a better attitude. Lunch will be ready in five minutes. You can fix yourself a plate when you're done."

"Do you need a hand picking out an outfit?" Adora adds smugly.

I bite my lip to keep from saying anything that'll have my head on a fucking chopping board, turn and walk away.

TWENTY

ADORA

Adora

His mother, Bianca, is kind. I'm not used to kindness from a parent. My mother left when I was young, and my father never really told me much about her. All I know is that I have her chocolate-brown eyes.

My sister and I have different mothers. Her mother was killed when she was six. I remember her more than my own because I was a little older, and I recall that she never liked me. And as a child, having the only mother figure you know not like you does a lot to a person. It made me beg my father to take me with him when he left the house, and he barely liked me.

I vividly remember the day I took his life. It flashes through my head constantly. *Do I regret it?* That would be a hard no. To him, I ended up being a possession. Nothing more, nothing less. I honestly can't even remember the last time he told me he loved me or that he cared for me. If you're born a woman in his world, you were basically his slave. All he ever wanted was a son to carry on his name.

Sometimes when he would get drunk, I would try to stay as far away from him as possible, but I could hear him swearing my name from the other room. How he wished that my mother hadn't aborted the child before me because it would've been a boy. And how he thought I was a boy until the day I was born, and then I turned out to be a girl, and it was the biggest disappointment of his life.

It was hard to be a young girl growing up in a powerful family. The strange part of it all was that everyone wanted to be a part of it but me. I would've given anything to trade places with any one of my classmates. I never had friends over, and I never went to friends' houses. I went to school, and I came home. That was my life.

When I was sixteen, I grew boobs, and my

father's friends started to notice. And my father started to notice that they noticed.

I was officially a plaything.

"Adora, you have a sister, don't you?" I glance up from my glass of wine and give Bianca a nod. "I can't wait to meet her. Is she much younger than you?"

I don't want to tell this family anything about my sister, but they already seem to know so much, so what does it even matter? It's not like she wants me in her life anyway. She blames me for what happened to our father, when really, she should be thanking me that she didn't end up the way I did. Now she gets to live a beautiful life in a privileged school. She gets to hang out with her friends and not worry about the fucked-up life we grew up in.

"Yes, but she lives back in Italy, and she goes to school there. I'm not sure if she wants to travel to America." His mother nods and then starts putting sauce followed by cheese on the pizza, and hints of garlic. And I wonder if this is what his life was like growing up. A mother in the kitchen cooking for them, caring for them, loving them. How lucky were they?

"I knew your father." The wine glass pauses before it touches my lips. I should've expected it since she was married to one of the bosses. She was bound to come across almost everyone at some point. "I didn't like him."

"I didn't like him either." I finish the glass of wine, and she offers me a small smile.

"I was actually surprised to hear he had girls. And your mother, I remember her as well. You have the same eyes, did you know?"

I give her a small nod and reach for the bottle to refill my glass.

We both turn as Joey walks into the room. He pulls out the stool two down from me, to make sure he isn't sitting next to me, and reaches for the bottle of water on the counter.

His mother smacks his hand away and tsks him.

"Mumma, I'm down, I'm here." He glances at me before he looks back at his mother. "Even when I don't want to be."

Burn! I know that's directed at me.

"I'm cooking you both lunch today and then you're going away for the weekend. Do you hear me, Joey?"

What? I sit there in shock. This is news. She didn't mention this at all when she was talking to me. When I look at Joey, I see he's as stunned as I am.

"I'm not going anywhere, I have to work," Joey

replies, but his mother shakes her head as if his words mean nothing.

"That's nice that you think you have a say in this, Joey. You're going away. This marriage *will* work. And to top it off, you *will* be nice to your new wife. Do. You. Understand. Me?"

I notice as Joey puts his hands on his lap, pinches his legs, then rubs it out.

"I have the bookstore," I add with a shrug.

Joey nods his head. "Yeah, she can't leave that."

Maybe he's just mean when he's drunk?

"I spoke to Lucas today, Adora. He said he has that all handled and that you shouldn't worry about a thing." Bianca looks to Joey. "Your brother agrees with me, so don't argue with me, son."

I'm not sure what else we can say.

We sit there like scolded children as Bianca cooks the pizza and passes her son a glass of wine.

"Neither of you have asked where you're going. Aren't you even the slightest bit curious?"

"No," Joey replies, then takes a long gulp of his wine.

I say nothing.

Bianca smiles. "You're off to Italy."

I can't even respond.

Italy is the last place I want to go.

It's a place that holds a lot of dark memories for me.

She probably thought it would be a smart idea to send me there, that maybe I could see my family, my sister, but my hands start shaking and somehow, I manage to hide them under the counter before Bianca sees them, but Joey catches the movement. His eyes swing to where my hands are closing into fists so tight my fingernails dig into my skin, but just as I'm about to draw blood, his voice stops me.

"We don't want to go to Italy, Mother. Bora Bora, on the other hand, could be nice."

I've always wanted to go there. I want to offer him a smile for his small act of kindness, but as I look at him, I can see that behind those icy blue eyes, he wants to murder me.

"And cancel tonight. No visitors. That can wait until we return."

"YOU CAN LEAVE NOW. I'm sure there's someone else you'd rather be seeing than sitting here in my kitchen." His mother has just left and advised us that tomorrow is when Joey and I are leaving for a vacation. He clearly doesn't want to be anywhere near me.

"And where am I meant to go, Joey?" I ask, feeling exasperated, tired, and completely over just about everything. Saying Becca's name accidentally is seeming like the worst thing I could have ever done, and he is one hundred percent going to hold it against me for the rest of my life.

He throws his hands up in the air. "I thought you'd want to go see your *little girlfriend.*"

"You told me I had to live with you, did you not?" I toss back the last sip of wine left in my glass before looking back at him.

"I did, and that hasn't changed. You will live here because you're my wife, regardless of whether we like it or not." He gets up from the stool at the kitchen counter. I watch as he walks past the blue bookcase, the one he said I can turn into my own private shelves, before he glances back at me. "If you fuck her, I'll kill her." And then he walks off after dropping that bomb on me.

I never intended to see Becca again. I'd planned to put her in my past and try to focus on the now.

Gathering my purse and keys, I don't even bother walking up to the bedroom before I leave. I drive straight to my happy place—my bookstore—and as I walk up to the door the 'Open' sign is clearly displayed out the front. I wasn't going to open it today, but Lucas said he had it covered. When I enter, there's a woman behind the counter who's leaning over it, tapping away on her phone. Her complexion is dark, her hair in braids, and her smile is bright when she looks up to greet me. "Hey, how are you today?" she chirps. I'm too stunned to speak. "Are you after any particular romance genre? We have a wide variety, and I am sure something to please."

"Arranged marriage." I don't know why I said that. Maybe I should read more books on it to give me a better perspective on my situation.

"O.M.G. I've just started reading a book that just came in. It's not arranged marriage, but it is about a marriage that's broken, and it's a must-read."

"Do you read often?" I have to know because that one book makes me wonder.

"My profession really didn't guide me in the way of books, so I guess my life is like one of these romance novels, only a little more fucked-up." I'm still standing just inside the door as I watch her talk animatedly.

"But I downloaded this app. I'm sure you've probably heard of it, it's quite popular. It's called

TikTok. Well, anyway... I landed on this BookTok side of things where all these women make these amazing videos about their books, and they just manage to grab these perfect parts that make you go 'oh my gosh, I have to read that.'" She shrugs. "So, yeah, that's why I picked up my first book, and now I'm here." She places her phone down on the counter. "Anyway, my name's Merci. Let me know if you need me." She turns around, reaches for a book, and opens it to a bookmarked page.

"You aren't meant to be here." We both turn at the sound of Lucas' voice as he enters with Chanel.

"Last time I checked, you aren't the boss."

"How are you?" Chanel asks, stepping up closer to me and placing her hand on my arm. She's kind, though she's a little rough around the edges. Considering she has to deal with Lucas on a daily basis, that's probably not such a bad thing. The ring on her finger glints under the bookstore's light. When they get married, I bet it won't be a shitshow like mine was.

"Oh, do you know each other?" the woman behind the counter asks.

Lucas smiles before he answers, "This is your boss."

"Ohhh."

"Merci, meet Adora. Adora, this is Merci."

Merci gives me a smile before she steps around the counter and offers me her hand. "I'm sorry I didn't realize who you were. Your shop is absolutely beautiful."

"It's fine. I enjoyed listening to you talk so animatedly about books. It's a passion all women should experience."

"Yes, passion, that's the word, right? How did it go last night? Did you two have a lot of passion? Or did you just fuck like dirty animals?" Lucas asks, his eyes boring into mine.

Chanel hits Lucas' arm for speaking like that, but I simply shrug. Lucas' words don't bother me anymore.

"He didn't even come home, so who knows who he fucked like a *dirty animal*," I reply.

Merci coughs and walks away.

I don't blame her.

TWENTY-ONE

JOEY

"Fuck! You look like absolute shit," Keir comments, ever so kindly, from the middle of my living room.

"Thanks, thanks a lot," I mumble. I close my eyes but snap them open when he kicks my foot. He's standing directly over me now.

"Mother said you two are going on a vacation. That it is needed. And, frankly, I agree with her. Look at the fucking state of you. Since when do you mope around like a fucking bitch? Get the fuck off the couch and be a fucking man." His words don't affect me that much because, clearly, he doesn't understand what it's like to be married to someone who doesn't want you. The woman he was engaged to before Sailor wanted him. She almost killed Sailor to be with him. So, when he says shit like that, the only thing I can do is shake my head and hope he goes away soon.

"I am a fucking man. You don't understand what it's like to marry a fucking lesbian."

"How do you know she's a lesbian?" he asks stupidly, catching my attention long enough to look up at him.

"You were with me that first day we went to see her, correct? When we walked in, and she had another woman's head between her legs? I mean, I wasn't seeing things. I wasn't on a movie set. You did see the same fucking thing as me, unless you are blind."

"Of course, I saw the same thing, dipshit, but have you stopped to consider that she also likes men?"

"She likes that *one* woman." That's pretty much all I know. *Does she like men too?* I have no idea as I haven't cared enough to ask her.

"Get the fuck off this couch and ask. We have a job to do."

The fun thing about what we do for work is it never stops. We are known to be cold-ass killers. But the truth of the matter is, we don't simply go around killing people for no reason. Unless you're Lucas.

The way you die by our hands is when you fuck us over.

We don't have the word forgiveness in our vocabulary. We weren't raised with it, so we don't know how to give it. And that's okay. This world isn't for everyone, and I completely understand that logic, but that's a reason the arranged marriages were always so successful. They were settled between two children who grew up in our world, who understood what was asked of them, what was expected of them, and what they will do for the family. They're not as frequent as they used to be when my parents were married, but they're still a thing. I'm living proof of that. Contracts have to be fulfilled. Otherwise, what honor do you have? And family is all about honor.

We pull up in front of Lucas' club to find him standing out front, his foot tapping impatiently as he waits for us. He offers me a sly smile, and I know he's going to say something to piss me off because that's who he is. He likes to ruffle feathers because his are hardly ever ruffled.

"Ran into your wife today." When I don't say anything, he continues, "Asked her how the fucking was going between you two. She wasn't forthcoming on the subject, so I'm going to ask you, cousin. How is it fucking someone who prefers to have pussy over cock?"

And that's all it takes for me to step toward him. I want to strangle him so that relentlessly smug expression vanishes from his face, but I have a feeling even as I'm choking him, he would still be smiling because that's the type of fucking asshole he is.

"Where my cock goes is none of your fucking concern, Lucas. You should know better."

Kier shakes his head and walks straight past us. And, of course, we're going to follow, like we always do.

Lucas waves his hand for me to go in first, and as I do, he whispers, "She's a little firecracker, that one. I'd watch out that she doesn't slit your throat when you sleep, just like she did to her father."

I should look into that. I mean, she told me she killed her father, but what was the reason behind it? Will she even tell me? Does Lucas know? Not sure I want to ask him to find out the truth.

"Joey?" I'm surprised to see an old school friend, Perry, sitting at a table inside. I don't particularly socialize with anyone other than my family any longer because it's safer that way. There's less betrayal, fewer people being killed.

His eyes brighten as he stares at me, hope shining

through them. "Joey, it is you. Fuck, help me get out of here."

Lucas and Keir both turn to me. Lucas starts to laugh, and it's then that Perry's face changes, and he realizes I'm not there to save him. It's like recognition floods his face, and he realizes who he's speaking to.

"I didn't think..." Perry shakes his head. "You didn't want nothing to do with this life in school." He's right, of course, but when my brother became boss, that was a different story.

"Things change, Perry. I changed." I don't even bother asking why he's here, tied to a chair in the back room of Lucas' club because I already know the answer. There are only one or two reasons they would be back here, and it's usually to do with money. Perry liked flashy things back in the day when we were in school, so I have a feeling that hasn't changed the older he's gotten, especially by the looks of his Gucci shirt.

"He told me everything I needed to know," Lucas tells me.

Perry goes to cut him off, but he doesn't get a chance because I raise my gun and shoot him directly between the eyes. His head lolls back, blood and brain matter splatters everywhere, and Lucas swears. He shakes his head because he was an idiot for standing too close.

"Next time, don't bring dipshit when he hasn't gotten laid," Lucas says to Keir before he walks off, leaving my brother and me standing there with Perry's lifeless body.

Kier looks at me. "You better come back from this fucking holiday ten times better." He shakes his head and walks off the same way Lucas did, throwing over his shoulder, "And fuck your damn wife."

TWENTY-TWO

ADORA

We boarded a private plane this morning to take us to our destination. I can't say I've been on one until today. Joey has hardly spoken to me, and we're already hours into our flight. It's awkward. He didn't come home again last night, and this time I didn't sleep on the couch, instead choosing his bed. And when I woke, his side wasn't even touched.

I had heard the door slam early this morning and then his heavy footsteps as he entered the room, still dressed in the outfit he left in yesterday.

"Do you plan to talk to me?" His eyes are closed in his seat, but I know he's not asleep. "Not sure how this vacation is meant to go if you plan on not speaking to me."

"Do you like cock?" His eyes open, finding mine already on him.

"W-What?" I stutter, completely caught off guard by the question.

He's asking me this now.

"Do you like cock or… is it only pussy that does it for you?" I realize I still haven't answered him as his eyes search my face for the truth.

"I've been with both men and women if that is what you're asking." He doesn't blink, doesn't even move, he simply stares at me. "Did you think I don't like cock?"

"It's hard to see how you can like cock when the only person you look at with interest is a woman."

He isn't lying, I can see why he would think that, at least since he's known me. But I also look at him with interest, but he's too stubborn and blind to see it. His anger clouds everything, and I guess I'm the reason he's angry in the first place.

Maybe I need to try harder, which is a difficult thing for me to do, but I have to be willing to try.

"I find you attractive," I admit, but it doesn't seem to soften him any. He blinks at me, and blinks again, as if he doesn't quite understand what I'm saying. "I can't say I would've given you a chance, Joey, if this thing wasn't forced on us." I wave my hand between us, taking a deep breath before I continue, "I would either be single or with Becca right now. I'm not gonna lie to you and say I don't have feelings for her because I do. But I've also told her that we can't be together because I have to try with you, but you're not making it easy for me to try."

He pinches his bottom lip before his teeth come out and scrape it. His eyes are still locked on mine, and I'm waiting for his response. For some reason, this conversation is making me anxious.

"If I ask you a question, will you answer it truthfully? "

He gives me a simple nod in reply.

"Do you find me attractive?"

At first, I think he's going to ignore me and not answer. He takes a moment to rub the scruff on his chin. It's only a few days old, but it gives him an edgier appearance, one that I quite enjoy looking at.

"I like my women with a bit more meat on their bones." His words shock me, but they shouldn't really because he's mentioned this fact to me before. I just didn't think he'd be so blunt and cavalier about it, not after what I just shared.

I turn my face away from him, not even bothering to say anything else, but then he speaks again,

"Yes, Adora, I do find you attractive, despite how much I hate you."

My mouth wants to lift in a smirk. He could've lied, and I'm not even sure if he is really telling the truth, but I have a feeling he is.

"Thank you."

"You're not welcome."

The plane flies over crystal clear water and beaches with white sand, and I wonder what it's going to be like over the next few days stuck on an island with a man who thinks I'm attractive but who can't stand me.

I guess I can try to work with the attraction thing for now.

THE BUNGALOW which is situated on stilts over the water is out of this world. It's perfect. I come from a life of luxury, but my luxury was stuck in my home. I didn't travel much when I was younger, even now I don't really go anywhere. And, yes, I like flashy things. I'm used to them, but I can live without expensive baubles. The clothes I wear usually come from the thrift shop. The only designer thing I own is something my father gave to me when I was thirteen.

He said it was my mother's, and now, it's all I have left of either of them.

A king-size bed dominates the inside of the bungalow. It looks soft as a cloud. A two-seater couch sits in front of a wall of windows that opens out onto our deck, which juts out over the ocean. This is where Joey is currently sitting, with his feet hanging over the edge, a bottle of whatever his preferred poison is today sitting next to him, and probably a sour expression on his face. He hasn't spoken to me since we arrived.

I get changed into a bikini, leaving my things all over the bed. I didn't know what to pack, so I brought a few pieces of everything. When I walk out onto the deck, I stand directly next to Joey, but he doesn't glance my way or even care that I'm standing there. He simply lifts his bottle to his lips and takes a long drink.

Fuck him.

I dive straight into the ocean, the water warm on my skin. And for a fraction of a second, I think about not coming up for air. I haven't made this easy on him, but he hasn't made this easy on me either.

How am I meant to open up to someone—to even grow to love him—when I want someone else at the same time? Sometimes the heart is a fickle bitch, and you just have to go with your head.

I surface, gasping for air, and then swim to the edge where his feet are dangling in the water. I stop just shy of touching him and glance up, but he's already looking down at me, those icy blue eyes locked on me like he's trying to work something out.

"Come for a swim."

He shakes his head once, stands, then goes inside.

This can't be how our vacation will be the whole time, can it? With him walking away every time I get close. Ignoring me every chance he gets.

Getting out of the water, I head inside to the bathroom, where I find him undressing, the shower already running. He glances up to see me behind him through the mirror. He's gloriously naked. I'm not complaining, he's incredibly nice to look at.

"Is this your plan?" I reach for the bottle of alcohol he brought in with him, lift it to my lips, and take a swig. "This needs to work between us, Joey, so stop fucking walking away from me and be a man."

He grinds his teeth at the words *be a man*. They agitate him. Good! At least I know he has other feelings besides constant disapproval.

"You are my wife, correct?" he snips at me.

I nod and look down at the simple band on my finger. It's nothing flashy, but it does its job of letting others know I'm his.

"I am," I confirm, then peer back up at him with confusion written all over my face.

"So a good wife pleases her husband, wouldn't you agree?" His gaze doesn't drop as he stares at me, but mine does because I see a small movement, and I notice his cock is getting hard.

"Please?" I ask, hiding my irritation and playing along. "In what way would you like to be pleased, Joey?"

"Well, you see, I'm a bit old-fashioned. And my cock here..." he motions to his cock, which is very hard now, "... hasn't had anyone's lips or cunt wrapped around it since the day I walked into your bookstore and saw you fucking someone else. And I would say that's a bit unfair to me, wouldn't you? Considering you've had others?"

"That's funny since you agreed to side pieces, and now you want traditional."

"I'm allowed to change my mind," is all he replies.

"Are you asking for sex, Joey?" *Is it really so hard for him to just come out and say it?* "If you want to fuck me, use your fucking words."

He cracks his neck from side to side, then turns around and steps into the shower. His hands run through his curly hair, down his chest, then stop suddenly. When his eyes spring open again, they lock on me.

"This is our honeymoon, is it not? People fuck on their honeymoons."

"I didn't think you'd want to fuck me. You know... considering I'm not your type."

"Fuck off, *darling*." His tone is filled with venom but has an underlying sarcastic tone as well.

Would I be considered a good wife if I walked out of here, went to that fruit platter that's sitting on the desk and grabbed the knife, then came back in here and just cut him? Then watched the blood fall to the floor as it mixes with the water on its way down the drain? Because the way this is going, that's exactly what I want to do right now—cut him open and watch him bleed.

Instead, I put my big girl panties on—or so the saying goes—and I start to remove my bikini. He doesn't notice because his eyes are closed, and his head is leaning against the wall as the hot water streams down his face. When I'm naked, I step in under the water, my front to his back, and he stiffens as he feels me behind him, but he doesn't move away.

Maybe he should, considering my thoughts about him only a moment ago.

I take two heavy breaths in and out, and on the third, I lift my hands and touch his naked waist. His breathing picks up, but he remains still. Inching my hand around just a little bit farther, I explore his perfect body. I move upward, my fingers roaming along his washboard abs to his chest until I get to his neck. I give it a little squeeze and push my body fully against his so he can feel every inch of me from behind.

"You're about to get hurt," he growls, but he still doesn't move. "You should step away now."

I should listen to his threat, but I don't.

Because, you know, good wife and all.

My hand that has been sitting on his waist drops a little lower through his manicured pubes until it reaches the base of his cock. He sucks in a breath as my fingers wrap around the shaft, and I feel myself getting wet between my legs at his reaction.

My body stays pressed against his, and I'm waiting for him to push me away, but he does nothing, simply stands there, statue-like. I have to pause to make sure he's breathing because he's so quiet.

"Darling, you don't know what you just did."

Well, doesn't that sound like another delicious

threat, and with a few swift movements, my hands have dropped and he's facing me, both our hands down by our sides. When I look up at his eyes, I see hunger written all over his face.

His hands remain clenched as if he's worried about what he might do with them. I've heard stories about the brothers. Joey was always considered the nice one—deadly, but nice. I suppose he was nice to begin with, that is until I crossed him. And I've crossed him in many ways.

You would think he didn't want me from every word that leaves his mouth, but his cock is telling me otherwise. Stepping another inch closer, I place my feet on top of his and wrap my hands around his neck, basically trying to crawl up his body. I hook one leg around his ass, then the other, and just when I think I'm about to drop to the shower floor, his hands grip both my ass cheeks and squeeze hard. So hard, I'm pretty sure his fingers are digging in and will leave bruises.

Goddamn, it feels incredible.

I need, no want, this man badly.

Our bodies are synced, and my pussy is throbbing so hard that I physically can't get any closer unless he is inside me.

The water falls over us, and his hair flops in his

eyes as I lean in to kiss him. But he pulls back, which makes me stop. I try again, and he does the exact same thing.

"We aren't here to make love. This is hate-fucking and that's all this will ever be. Do you fucking understand?"

Well, then.

Fuck him.

"Just fuck me already and get it over and done with."

Joey's hands release their hold, and I slide down his body until I'm standing. Then he walks out, leaving me in the rapidly cooling water.

TWENTY-THREE

JOEY

Who the fuck says that? Why on earth would you say that as you're climbing my fucking body, wanting me to stick my cock into your fucking cunt? I stormed out without even bothering to grab my towel.

She follows me out. I can hear her tiny little footsteps coming up behind me.

"Joey!" she screams, but I don't bother stopping. "Joey, are you a pussy cunt bitch?"

That makes me spin around and face her. "What the fuck did you just say?" I'm trying to keep my anger out of this situation, but I can't with her. She infuriates me on every level possible. I want to do things I know I shouldn't—yell obscenities, put my fist through the wall, pick up the closest thing and throw—but instead, I stand there taking in what's in front of me. Adora's hand is on her naked hip, which is pushed out to one side in a defiant stance. She doesn't give one damn fuck that she's completely bare in front of me. Fuck, I don't even care that I'm naked too. Most women try to cover themselves and regain some modesty while standing there, ready for a fight. But no, not her.

Adora's hair is dripping wet and dangling over her shoulders and the expression on her face is one of enraged fury. Her eyes pin me. They are that hard and flinty, her cheeks could not be any redder, and that body is so tense her muscles will be sore tomorrow.

I was hoping the woman I married would be calm and sweet, yet I'm stuck with the Devil herself.

What do they call a woman devil?

A she-devil?

A deviless?

"You heard me."

Against my better judgment, I walk over to her until we're nose to nose. "I like it better when you keep your mouth shut." She gives me an eye roll. "I don't intend to fuck my wife when she talks like that.

You *will* want me, *darling*. It's simply a matter of time."

Her hand lifts as if she's about to slap me, but instead, she grabs my face, eyes locked on me, before slamming her lips to mine.

I don't want pity sex.

I don't even want a pity fucking kiss.

I am *not* someone's sad fucking story.

So without letting it go too far, I push her away.

Adora grabs me tightly, and because I'm not kissing her back, she bites my lip until I taste my own blood. But she doesn't stop there. Her body is now pressed against mine, her mouth on me, and that's when I feel her start to move. My cock is hard as a rock, and she's grinding herself against me. Without thought, I open my mouth and her tongue slips inside. I can taste my own blood on her tongue, yet neither of us stops. I guess we're going through with this even though I want to pull away more than anything, but my body won't let me.

Her legs wrap around my waist again, and I hoist her up. Moving blindly, I slam her against the wall. Our lips break apart as she gasps, but her hands are still on my shoulders, nails digging into my flesh. Her breathing is heavy as she looks down between us.

Her hands are fast and frenzied as she reaches for my cock and lifts herself by her legs on my waist, positioning herself to sink down on me.

But I stop her.

"Tell me... do bad little *darlings* deserve cock?"

Adora bites her bottom lip and rolls it between her teeth. I wonder if she can taste the splatters of my blood that are still on her lips from where she bit me. What I really want is to wrap my hands around her throat and watch as her pretty red lips turn blue.

Hmm... I wonder if she would like that.

Possibly not.

"No, but your wife most certainly does."

Goddammit! I hate the fact that I like the sound of her calling herself my wife. I go to speak, but before I can, she pushes herself down while at the same time pushing me back, giving her more space, and then drops down ever so fucking slowly. And the moment I feel her—all of her—around my cock, I suppress a groan and know I'm not going to be able to stop.

I thought I could stop this.

But that's what fools tell themselves, right?

I hold on tight. "Is that what you're calling yourself now? My wife?"

"Just shut up and fuck me, Joey."

No woman has ever made me this mad and this fucking deliriously horny all at the same time. *How is that possible?* When I go to move her, she positions herself clinging to me with even more force. Her face buries into my neck, her legs wrap around my hips even tighter and knot at the back, and she clenches around my cock.

But she doesn't make a sound.

I want to hear those moans from her lips because I've heard them from a phone, and I sure as fuck know I can get them if I try hard enough.

"Maybe you should be a good little wife, instead of a slut for others." I slap her ass hard, and she yelps. The sudden jolt causes her to move her hips up and down, so I do it again, and she does the exact same thing. I start walking with her, holding her to me, and I have to remember not to come because every time her sweet pussy slides up and down, she clenches just that little bit tighter and rides me a little bit smoother.

I have to remember I hate her.

Despise the ground she walks on.

She pulls back, but she doesn't slow her movements. I almost trip over my own feet, while she acts like a koala, holding herself to me. Her back is arched, head now lifted, hair hanging down her back. As I step outside, her eyes are closed and her lips are parted, and I can still see the droplets of my blood there. I push her back against the glass wall, and she lets out another yelp and stops for a second. I watch her eyes scan around the other bungalows.

"Someone might see us." I lift a hand and touch a finger to her lips, smearing the blood. I wonder if it's all over my face as well since I can still taste it. I nip at her bottom lip and pull it between my teeth before I let it pop out. She tastes so fucking good.

"I guess I'll see what a good little slut you are."

Her eyes go wide, but I hold her against the glass as my hips start moving. She simply stares at me, her expression changing from being shocked to disgusted right before my eyes.

What did she expect me to say?

This is not a hearts-and-flowers fuck.

This is hard, fast, and with a care factor of zero fucks.

Her hand releases, and then she goes to slap me straight across my face and succeeds with a hard and fast strike. I throw my head back and laugh at her fucking audacity. She goes to do it again, but I capture her wrist mid-swing and hold it tight.

"Is this what you're into? Do you want me to slap you around like you're my good little slut, *darling*?"

"Get your cock out of me. *Now*," she seethes, and I smile at her fiery glare.

"With pleasure."

I lift her and take two steps back, then drop us both into the ocean.

TWENTY-FOUR

ADORA

"I'm still mad at you," I tell him.

He shrugs. "I'm furious too. But come on, I'll be the gentleman here and let you have your say first as to why you're mad at me."

"Because of what you did."

"Okay, since you can't form a coherent sentence, I guess that means I've fucked you senseless. I don't recall you coming because I sure fucking didn't. How about you continue to be senseless on your knees, I could do with some good head right now?"

I do just that but with one goal in mind.

Getting on my knees in front of him, I tilt my head to look up at him. His eyes are filled with venom, and it matches how I'm feeling inside.

"That's where you belong, my *darling*."

I pull his towel loose and his still-hard cock springs free. I admire it for a moment before hate fills me right back up to overflowing. Leaning forward, I grip his cock, place the tip in my mouth, and...

... I bite it.

He screams.

Loudly.

He flings me backward, but not hard enough to hurt me, and proceeds to cup his cock like it's a precious baby.

"Have you lost your goddamn mind?" he bellows, his eyes crazed as he looks at me for an explanation. "You fucking bit my cock."

I get back to my knees and say, "Good little slut, right?" I give him my best fuck-you smirk before I stand and turn to walk away from him, but he catches me by my waist and spins me back around. I hit his chest a few times to try and get away, but he pulls me close so my arms are trapped at my sides as he holds me hostage against his naked body. He can't throw me back in the water now unless he picks me up and carries me back outside.

My phone starts dinging, and I ignore it while still trying to wriggle my body as much as I can to get him off.

He growls as it starts ringing. "Turn that fucking

thing off. Who has a booty song as their ring tone anyway?" He lets me go and stalks off, still cupping his cock.

All I was trying to do was fuck him and look how that turned out.

When he returns, he's fully dressed. He doesn't say a word as he heads right out the door, leaving me here by myself.

Something he's become increasingly good at.

HE CAME BACK, eventually. We hardly spoke. Well, he didn't speak at all when I asked him if he wanted to share some steak with me. He grunted, and then I passed out on the couch, looking out through the open doors to the inky ocean and the black sky.

When I sit up, I find him already awake and dressed. He's sitting on the bed, food in front of him, as he does something on his phone.

No, hold up, that's not his phone. Managing to stand despite my exhaustion, I walk over to him and snatch *my* phone from his hand.

"What do you think you're doing?" I don't have a

passcode lock on it because I tend to forget it and my phone is always with me.

He picks up a piece of fruit and puts it in his mouth. "Who is Scott?" he asks.

A shiver takes hold of me at the sound of that name. I despise that name and all it entails.

"None of your business."

"You see, I think it is." He picks up another piece of fruit and holds it out to me. "Eat. You are way too skinny." I swat the fruit from his hand, making it fly across the room. He isn't bothered by my outburst, just reaches for another piece and does the same. "Now, I'll ask again… who is Scott?"

"Aren't you meant to be the nice one?" I ask with a huff. "Nice people do not go through each other's phones.

He moves and produces his own phone, offering it to me. "You want to go through mine?"

"No." A part of me does, I'm not going to lie. *What type of pictures does he have on it?*

"I can see you want to. Go ahead and take it. I did go through yours after all." I snatch it from his hand and pocket mine in my jean shorts as I open his. "Password."

"Twelve, ten." I snap my gaze to his. That's our wedding date. I don't bother saying anything as I enter it, and it unlocks. I flick straight to his camera reel and see pictures of his niece filling the gallery. The last few are of us on our wedding day. I zoom in and look at my face—it looks like I'm in pain. Like I don't want to be there. It's true, I didn't, but gosh. Getting out of his camera reel, I go to his messages. The first one is from Lucas, and it reads, *"Fucked her in the ass yet? We all know that's how you like it."* I almost laugh. There are several from Lucas—all taunts—with no replies from Joey.

Not much in here at all, so I close it and hand it back.

"Now, tell me who Scott is."

"You don't deserve to have that information." No one knows who he is, not even my best friend, and I intend to keep it that way for as long as possible.

"I'm your husband. If you're messaging some other guy, I should know."

My hands start fidgeting, and I hate that they do that when I get nervous. "You don't deserve to know," I scream.

"So not only are you wanting a woman, but you also want another man?" he asks, clearly irritated now.

"You don't deserve to know," I whisper this time.

Joey seems to get the hint and stands. "What are

we doing today?" His change of attitude surprises me, and his eerily calmness shocks me even more.

I'm not sure how to answer him. Do I avoid and say nothing or change as fast as he just did, so I decide on the safer option. "I want to try jet skiing."

"Done. Get changed." He grabs the empty plate and walks out.

Not bothering to close the door, I change into my bathing suit. He's seen it all anyway. When I turn around to reach for my swim top, his eyes are on me. He doesn't look away, nor does he seem to care that I just caught him staring. I reach for the strap and tie it around my neck, ever so slowly. Now is the time to let things go just as easily as he did for me.

I bite the inside of my cheek before I speak, "Can you help me?" I ask, turning around and pointing to the ties at the back of my swimsuit. I glance over my shoulder and see him walking toward me. His fingers brush my back, tickling, as he grabs each tie. His touch drags along my flesh and goosebumps take over my skin. He is slow, deliberate, and his breath wafts along my neck as he goes, making me shiver. I know if I glanced back at him, his face would be close to mine.

"Done?" I ask as I feel him tighten the ties.

His fingers stay on my back as he says, "Done."

He doesn't move, so I take the first step away. Though I'm not sure I want to.

"Have you been jet skiing before?" I ask, trying to break the tension between us.

He rolls his shoulders ever so slightly. "Yes. We should go." His hand grips mine and he slides our fingers together. The gesture is so normal, so gentle, that I find myself momentarily distracted before I find my voice again.

"I haven't been on one before. Can I ride with you?"

"Yes."

It doesn't take us long to get there. Joey takes us out onto the ocean, my arms wrapping around his waist as goes. I'm gripping on for dear life with how fast he's going, afraid at every bump I may very well fly off the back. We ride for what feels like forever and then he suddenly stops. My hands are sore from gripping onto him so tightly.

He turns around, but I can't see his eyes with his sunglasses covering them. "Your turn."

I shake my head vehemently. "No way, I'll kill us."

"Ha." I give him a skeptical look, and he shakes his head, a hint of a smile tugging at his lips. "You won't. Climb over me and sit between my legs." I stand on legs that feel like Jell-O and do just that, climb over him until his hands are on my sides, guiding me as he pulls me back down. I feel him behind me—all of him—as he slides forward to reach for the handles and starts explaining what to do. I'm so lost and confused because all my attention is focused on the feel of him. Everywhere.

"You want to go fast because the slower you go, the more you feel the waves."

"No, I want to go slow," I affirm, shaking my head.

"Trust me. It's smoother going faster." I place my hands on the handlebars and his cover mine. "I've got you," he promises as the engine starts. Then we're off, and he doesn't let go until I give him a nod. When he releases the handlebars, his hands come to my waist, gripping it before one hand slides around and hugs me to him. His fingers play with my skin, and it's so distracting that I start to slow down.

"Speed up," he instructs, and his fingers move lower. "Faster," he growls, and I turn the throttle a little bit more.

My hair, which was tied back, is whipping into my face as his hand drops to my bikini bottoms. I feel his fingers dip inside, then trail down until he reaches my clit, and my body jolts from the contact.

His finger slides between my folds, and he applies the perfect amount of pressure to make a moan escape my lips. It's not loud enough to hear over the engine, but he can probably feel the sound with how close he's settled against me. I open my legs wider, which is silly considering I'm straddling the seat, basically giving him permission, I suppose.

His other hand glides up my body, pulling my breast free and squeezing the nipple between his fingers, the other is still circling my clit. I start rocking ever so slightly, the jet ski slowing as I do.

"Faster," he says into the skin on my neck, and I almost don't hear him, but he pinches my clit with his fingers. "Faster."

And I go faster.

His fingers slide down until he's at my entrance, and I start grinding on his hand. I can feel his cock at my back getting harder with every movement of my hips. I want to stop driving. I want to stop so badly, but he keeps on telling me to go faster.

So that's what I do.

Obey.

Listen.

Learn.

He frees my other breast and pinches the nipple before he rolls it between his fingers as well.

Fuck.

Fuck.

Fuck.

"Stop," he orders.

My hands instantly release, and the jet ski slows to a stop.

I can't help myself. Suddenly, I'm not afraid that we're out in the ocean. I throw my leg over the seat and turn myself around, my body ignited absolutely everywhere as I reach for his cock and free it from his swim trunks. He pushes my hand away as soon as his cock his free, and I grip his shoulders, and he ever so slowly pulls me down. His eyes look haunted as I grip him.

I want to sink onto him, *need* to, but he doesn't let me. Gripping me tightly, so he has all the power until I am fully on him, a smug look sits on his face, but I am too needy to question it or care. He scoots forward, his hands disappearing from my body.

I hear the sound of the jet ski's engine, barely, but my hips are already moving. His mouth grabs hold of my nipple, and he sucks it before he does the same to the other. "Hold on." My hands grip around his neck, clinging to him as close as possible, our bodies almost one, mine slowly moving up and down just enough to feel the friction as we take off again.

He bites my shoulder as I fuck him, never once stopping even though we're in full view of anyone we might pass.

Our joining is powerful.

The wind is whipping through my hair, and I'm trapped between him and the handlebars, not able to go anywhere as he steers us.

"Fuck," I scream as I start to feel the build-up.

"Who is Scott?" he asks, but his voice sounds so far away with my heart beating so loudly in my ears.

"My father's acquaintance," I answer on a moan.

"What does he want with you?"

Oh my God. Oh my God.

I can't stop. I can't. This...

... is the best sex of my life.

How is that possible with someone you don't like?

His mouth finds my neck, and he sucks before he kisses it, never once slowing down as he drives.

"Adora."

"Hmm..."

"What does he want with you?"

"He wants me," I manage to say.

"Do you want him?"

"No."

The jet ski stops, but my hips do not.

"Do you want me, Adora?" He kisses my neck again, lavishing my most sensitive spot.

"Fuck, yes."

Joey's hand slides down my body to my ass, and he inserts a finger, ripping a scream from me as I come. "That's a good girl," he praises, removing his hand and gripping my hips and rocking them himself. I'm spent but, clearly, he is not. He keeps fucking me until he finds his own release, biting me again when he does.

I'm going to be covered in bruises, and I'm not sure I want to complain about it.

"That was..."

He starts to fix my top, covering my breasts back up, then pushes me up so his cock leaves me. He tucks himself back in and adjusts my bottoms, then turns me back around as if I am a toy.

"Drive us back." He doesn't sound cold, more demanding. I would think he was mad, but when his hands stroke my skin, I know he isn't. His mouth lands on my upper back and leaves little kisses all over it.

When we get back to shore, he lifts me and helps me off like he would a child. When the man from the jet ski rental company comes down to meet us, his eyes go to my neck, and I pull my hair free to cover it.

Joey just smirks before he reaches for me, and we leave.

"You want to keep the footage?" the guy asks avoiding eye contact with me.

What? My eyes go wide as I look back at Joey.

The bastard smirks.

"You didn't see the camera?"

"Camera?" I ask.

The guy nods, and his cheeks blush.

"Yes, I'll take it. And make sure any copies are destroyed. Otherwise, I may very well come back and kill you." I watch as the guy takes a deep breath and swallows before he hands over a flash drive with shaky hands. When he walks off, I look at Joey.

"Want to watch yourself come?"

"No."

"Why? I think I may very well put it on repeat. Best thing I've seen in a long time."

"Destroy it," I tell him, walking off as he slides it into his pocket.

"If you say so, wife."

TWENTY-FIVE

JOEY

It seems the way to make her talk is to make her come. Which I definitely don't have an issue with. I will gladly make her come any chance I get.

She steps out of the shower, a towel wrapped around her as she walks over to the bed where I'm sitting. She doesn't hesitate to push the book I was reading onto the bed and climb onto my lap.

"Scott was my father's associate," she tells me hesitantly. I can tell how nervous she is because her eyes go down to my stomach, and she runs her fingers along the trail of hair I have there. "I was given to him as a gift." My chest constricts at those words, but I remain silent, and her eyes lift to find mine. "I don't want Scott. I detest Scott, but I have to be nice to him."

None of those words make any sense.

"How old were you?" I ask, even though I know I won't like her answer.

She bites her bottom lip. "Sixteen."

"And you..."

"Yes, we had sex. He was a little younger than my father."

"Did he rape you?" I press, my hands clenched at my sides. Rape is a no-go for me. I fucking hate rapists.

"No, but it was definitely close to that. The older I get, the more I see it for the manipulation that it was." She moves and lays her head on my chest, her warm body covering mine, the towel and my boxer briefs are all that separate us.

She stays quiet and listens to my heartbeat for a few minutes before she speaks again, "My father did that... passed me around. But he did it in a smooth way, so I didn't realize what he was doing until it was too late."

"Is that why you killed him?" If she hadn't already done the deed, I certainly would have for this. The man deserved everything he got and more —death is too easy a punishment for someone like him.

"Partly, but that's not the main reason." Her

head moves, and her chin comes to rest on my chest. "It's why I didn't want to marry you. Because even in death, he still gets to choose who he passes me to."

Fuck.

I get it now.

"I'm sorry," I tell her, my tone softening. And I am sorry that her life is still being controlled by a dead man.

"I wanted to fight you at every turn, but then I came to realize that you aren't like the others. Even when you were angry, you still cared. Believe me when I say they didn't." She turns her head back, so her cheek is against my chest again. "When I moved to America, I met a girl, and she kissed me one night when we were out. And I liked it, a lot. I could take control of the situation with women. No woman can boss me around. Not like a man can."

"You don't have to live with me if you don't want to," I say, realizing I manipulated and bossed her into doing exactly that.

"It's fine, Joey. I like your place." I reach for her hair, and my fingers stroke through it, feeling her relax against me.

"I like both men and woman. I didn't choose Becca, she just happened to be there at that right time. I was in a mood, she was available."

"You want her, though." I know she does.

"I want you too." Her eyes find mine, and her chin rests on my stomach. "I find you very attractive, Joey Rossi, but I also find her attractive." I take a deep breath, trying to ignore my resentment from the second half of her admission and focus purely on what she said first.

That she wants me.

Isn't this what I've been waiting for?

"I don't approve of you being with her while you're married to me." That will *not* happen. She is *mine*, and no one else gets to have her while she's with me. I'll never have a sidepiece, and neither will she. Does that make me as bad as her father? Am I a manipulating, controlling bastard? A part of me doesn't even care if I am because the simple fact is, *she is mine.*

"I wouldn't do that to you. I mean, I would if you were a cheating asshole. Why would I stay faithful? That's just stupid. And I'm sorry, but I am not like your mother."

She's talking about how my father cheated on my mother throughout their marriage, and my mother stayed with him and remained faithful until the day he died. He didn't deserve her, or her loyalty, he deserved nothing from her.

"I'm glad you aren't like her," I say, smiling, and she smiles back. A real one. Bright and content, making her glow.

"I like her. Do you think she likes me?" Adora asks, and the look in her eyes is the sweetest she's given me. That's all I want to see now. "My mother ran off when I was young, and my sister's mother hated me. All I had was my father, who saw me as a possession because I wasn't a boy."

"She loves you. If you had flicked through my messages, you would have seen that she messages every day to check on you."

"You can give her my number," she says, her smile growing.

"I will, but don't blame me when you become best friends with her and then you can't get rid of her."

"She has Sailor."

"No, Keir has Sailor."

"Are your mother and Sailor not close?" she asks, tilting her head, and my hand brushes her hair over her shoulder with the movement.

"They are, but I have a feeling you two will have more in common."

"Joey."

"Hmm..."

"I'm ready for round two." She sits up and removes her towel, dropping it to the floor beside us. Then she scoots backward until she reaches my briefs, freeing my cock. "Do you want me on my knees, Joey, like a good girl?"

Fuck. My cock strains, and her eyes flick to it with a smile. She gets off the bed and drops to her knees. I reach for my phone as she clasps my cock in her small hand, then her mouth covers the tip, her tongue flicks out, and her eyes meet mine.

"Stay still." I unlock my phone and take a photograph.

"See what a good girl you are? Now I can set that as my screen saver." She doesn't tell me no, and you can't see my cock, just her eyes looking up with something in her mouth.

It's beautiful, just as she is.

Fuck.

Fuck.

I'm going to fall in love with my wife.

And I'm not sure how I feel about that.

TWENTY-SIX

ADORA

Every day for three days straight, we fucked, we ate, and we slept together. We spoke often but kept things basic, discussing things like his brother, his family, and my love for books. He tells me how much he despises but respects Lucas. That his brother is a man he respects not just because they are related but for who he is as a person.

He reads a lot, but we don't have the same taste in reading material. So I gave him one of the books I love, and he devoured it. It's called *The Sweet Gum Tree* written by Katherine Allred. When he finished, he sat there speechless and then offered me a smile.

"I can see the appeal."

"Wait until you get to the dirtier books." I offered him a wink. Then we left to head home.

Now we're sitting in a car on our way back to his place. I guess I should say *our* place.

"Your leg is bouncing."

I glance down as his hand slides over my thigh, and he gives it a comforting squeeze.

"It's a lot," I tell him honestly. "We're no longer in our bubble, and this is going to be an adjustment." He pulls me to him, lifting me easily and placing me on his lap. His hand gently pushes my hair back from my face.

"When you need our bubble, just say, 'bubble.'" His words make me smile.

"And what do you supply in that bubble?" I ask, pulling at his shirt.

"Whatever it is that you need. Me, peace, you name it, I'll supply it."

I hum in answer, sinking into his embrace. "And what if I require something a little more?" Turning on his lap, my knees rest on either side of him. The car comes to a stop, and he leans forward, his hand threading through my hair as he pulls me to him. His lips touch mine ever so softly before they smash onto mine with dominance, our mouths dancing together in a bruising kiss.

It's a dance that only skilled people should do—

fuck, kiss, kill—yet here we are tangoing with our mouths as if we do it every day.

Joey sure does know how to tango.

"Aww, look... they finally learned to like each other." We break apart to see Lucas at the door. When I peek out, I see several people there, even his mother. I move off Joey's lap and scoot to my side of the car, so we aren't even touching.

"What the fuck are you doing here?" Joey asks Lucas as he gets out of the car. He shuts his door and comes around to mine, opening and holding out his hand for me to take. "Are you nervous?" He nods to my legs which are still jittery, and I shake my head, taking his offered hand. "They're here to welcome us home. It's a lunch."

Oh.

Everyone is making their way inside as I get out of the car. The driver grabs our bags as we follow them in.

"So, how did the fucking go? Good, I'm assuming?" Lucas asks as we enter.

I swat his chest and walk past him. Lucas doesn't bother me—I'm used to him—but he seems to grate on Joey's nerves, which, in turn, makes Lucas want to do it even more.

"Lucas," Joey's mother warns.

Lucas holds up his hand and grips Chanel to him for protection, standing behind her and wrapping his arms around her middle. "I'll behave, Mrs. Rossi," he says politely and then kisses Chanel's neck.

The doorbell rings, and Keir moves past us to get it, coming back with several pizza boxes and bringing them to the table. Joey takes our bags and puts them at the bottom of the steps as we make our way to the dining area, where everyone's taking a seat and talking. Chanel sits with Keir's daughter in her lap, whispering to her and making her laugh. Sailor sits next to me while their son sleeps in his stroller.

"I've always wanted to go to Bora Bora. Was it magical?" Sailor asks, smiling.

"It was," I tell her truthfully. "I've never had a vacation like that before in my life."

"Keir is too busy to go, and he would hate it if I went without him." Keir doesn't say anything, just listens to his wife.

"What activities did you do?" his mother asks. "Scuba diving? Did you see any turtles?" his mother says with excitement. "Oh, what about jet skiing?"

I glance over to Joey to see him lower his head with a slight smirk on his face.

"Your cheeks are red. Why are your cheeks red?" Lucas asks me. "You never get embarrassed."

"Shut up, Lucas." Joey's hand taps on the table.

"Did you do something dirty on the jet ski, book-store girl?" I can feel my cheeks burning, knowing they're bright red right now. Lucas just doesn't seem to care.

"We did, in fact, go jet skinning," Joey adds. "Among other things."

"So, you two are doing well, then?"

"Of course, they are, they're fucking," Lucas adds with no regard to Bianca and the children in the room.

"I had..." Chanel covers the little girl's ears, "...sex with you, and I hated you at the time."

"Pssh, that's different. I knew for the both of us it was just a matter of time until you realized I was your everything," Lucas replies with his eyes locked onto Chanel's.

"The marriage is a success then," Keir says more like a question, looking at his brother.

Joey doesn't say anything but grips my leg under the table, his hand sliding up until his fingers play at the hem of my denim skirt.

"I would say so," their mother adds. From the look on her face, she couldn't be any happier.

Lucas keeps on talking about things we have no idea about. Sailor talks to Chanel and me while his mother pours drinks. She gets to me and places a kiss on my cheek before setting the wine glass in front of me and continuing around the table.

"Took her a while longer to warm up to me," Sailor leans in to tell me with a smirk. I smile and huff a laugh, but really, all I can think about is how his hand is sneaking up my skirt even farther.

"Hmm," I answer, not really being able to say much right now.

Keir calls Joey's name, but Joey doesn't remove his hand. He simply answers him by looking his way. His fingers trail all the way up until he gets to my panties. I suck in a breath as he ever so lightly pushes them to the side and slips a finger inside me.

"I need you back tomorrow," Keir tells him.

"I'll be back," Joey answers, his eyes not on me but his fingers in me.

"Joey," I whisper, leaning into him. Everyone's eyes fall on me. "Stop."

He all but smirks as he leans down and kisses my cheek, then whispers in my ear, "But I love the face you make when you come. It's officially my favorite thing."

Someone coughs next to me, and I know it's Sailor.

"Joey," I groan. My hips move, but I try to keep

them still. His mother is across from us, and the last thing I should be doing is coming on her son's fingers while we sit around with the family eating lunch.

Joey doesn't seem to care, though.

A loud knock comes on the door, and everyone stills. Even Joey's hand pauses.

"Are you expecting a delivery?" Joey asks me.

When I don't answer, he applies pressure to my clit.

"No."

"Okay." He pulls his hand away and puts it on the table. Reaching for his drink, he lifts it to his lips before taking a sip. I watch in fascination as he puts it down, his forearms flexing and his tattoos on display as his sleeves are rolled up. He turns to look at me, puts his finger in his mouth, and cleans it with his tongue.

I want to gasp, but I do nothing as he pushes his seat back and stands. He steps directly behind me and leans down to kiss my hair. "I'll be back." Then he walks off.

"This is nice to see, considering where you were over a week ago at the wedding," Sailor remarks, the shock clear in her expression.

"Yes, it's refreshing. He's happy, and that's all we

want for him is to be happy," his mother says, as I glance around the table and see all eyes on me.

Keir is watching me, assessing me like he always does.

Lucas sits there smirking—it wouldn't be Lucas if he wasn't smirking or making fun of something.

The women offer me soft smiles.

"Yes, we clashed at first, that's for sure," I agree, and I find myself smiling too. "It's gotten better, though. We just had to jump over a few hurdles."

"All the best relationships have hurdles."

"Adora," Joey yells, and everyone turns to see him standing in the entryway, his jaw ticking and anger flashing over his face.

What the hell happened!

Pushing my chair back, I stand immediately, already moving toward him before he speaks again, "You should come here. Now."

The room has gone eerily silent.

My bare feet carry me until I'm standing in front of Joey. I reach out for his hand to calm him down, but he takes a step back. When he does, I look around him to see who's at the door.

Becca. Her hands are clasped together at her front, and her head is down.

"Becca?" As I take her in, my eyes widen with

confusion. "Are you okay?" She looks paler than usual. Frightened?

Her eyes glance up at me. "I've been trying to reach you. This was the last place I could think of where I might find you. I've been to your shop, but you haven't been there. I'm so sorry." I go to step toward her, but Joey's hand grips my hip, keeping me in place.

Becca sees the movement and bites her lip. "I shouldn't have come." She shakes her head, and I watch as she turns and walks down the stairs, unsure of what just happened or how to feel about it. I stay where I am, Joey's hand still holding me. When I glance over my shoulder to look at him, he doesn't seem any less upset, the anger is emanating from him.

"This is your last chance to say goodbye. *Nothing more.* If any part of your body touches her, I'll kill her." He drops his hand from me and strides back to the dining area. I hear soft voices as I stand there questioning myself about what to do.

I don't know why she's here.

And because she did come here, my husband is now furious at me.

Reaching for my phone, I unblock her number and see all her messages come through. They are all desperately asking me to meet up, saying that she needs to see me, almost to the point of begging. Sliding my phone back into my pocket, I walk back into the dining area and take my seat next to Joey. He doesn't look at me, but his hand finds my thigh, and he offers me a small squeeze. My body relaxes at his reassurance, feeling like I can breathe again.

"Your girlfriend showed up?" Lucas asks with a smirk.

Joey turns and picks up a bread stick and hurls it at him.

Lucas laughs as it hits him in the face.

And for the rest of the day, we don't speak of Becca again.

TWENTY-SEVEN

JOEY

Lunch went well, all things considered. My mother made sure the refrigerator was stocked before she walked out the door. Lucas was the next to leave, thank fucking God. And Sailor and Adora have gone to the kitchen to get more wine, leaving me alone with Keir.

"She makes you happy?" he asks.

"That's hard to say, but so far, we're getting along."

"You seem smitten with her, and I know what smitten looks like. I've been there... I am there."

"I don't love her," I point out.

"Yet," Keir adds, lifting a glass to his lips. "It could be worse. You two could have remained as you were and never got along. This way has a better outcome."

"What do you know of her father?" I ask the question I've wanted to ask all night.

"Not much. Why?"

"He used to hand her out to his friends. Did you know about that?"

"He what?" Keir's expression shifts clearly confused but catching where the conversation is heading. "As in..."

"She hasn't divulged everything yet, but yes, that *is* how I'm taking it."

"What did she tell you?"

"A man was calling her, and I asked who he was. She told me after..." I don't add how I got that information out of her by making her come. "That he was a man who she met through her father."

"Is that why she killed him?"

"I believe so."

"You should ask her. It would be safer for you to know. You don't want to piss her off and not wake up the next day due to a knife being lodged in your throat," he jokes. I don't laugh, though. "And the woman?"

I glance toward the kitchen where Adora is helping with tidying up.

"Do you think she loves her?"

"I think she was close, but it's hard to tell with her." I grip the glass in my hand but don't drink from it. "She wants her more than she wants me."

"But she does want you," Keir states without an ounce of doubt, and I wish I had that same confidence in this situation. "I can see it. We all saw it. And just before, she chose to come back to sit next to you, not chase after the woman. You've got to take that as a win."

"She did." I nod because I took note of that too.

"So have a little faith. There is hope there after all."

"It's time we go," Sailor says as she walks into the room.

Adora helps her get the kids ready and carries their bags outside.

Keir's hand lands on my back.

"Ask questions. Get to know her. It's the only way forward."

We watch them leave, and as soon as the door shuts behind us, Adora looks at me pleadingly. "I need to talk to her. She seemed worried and not like herself." I know who she's talking about, and I say nothing as she steps up to me. "I like you, Joey. I do.

One day, I could even love you. But right now, I need to know what's wrong with Becca. I want you to stay by my side as I call her, so you can see that I have no ill intentions."

"You aren't allowed to go back to her," I tell her, and it's like some sort of reflex action, but then I realize it's more about protecting what's mine. I grip her waist again, and her eyes glance down to my fingers, then back up to my face.

"I don't intend to. As I said, I'm worried. I promise that's all." She reaches up, running her fingers through my curls, and my arm circles her waist.

"We can wait. How about you take me to bed?" she suggests, and a small smile plays on her lips. As tempting as she is, I don't want to stray from the subject until I know she really wants that and isn't worrying about something else or thinking about that woman rather than concentrating on me. Yeah, call me selfish, I don't give a fuck. When my woman comes, I want to be the only thing she thinks about.

"Call her."

Adora shakes her head slowly, and the look in her eye answers my concern before she does. "It's waited all this week, so it can wait one more night.

Now, how about we go up and christen our bed? We haven't done that yet."

"Now you're talking my kind of language." My lips brush hers as I pick her up and forget all about the bullshit thoughts I previously had. Instantly, her legs wrap around my waist and her arms wind around my neck.

"It's a bit unfair, don't you think, that you got to play with me, and I didn't get to play with you?" I take the first step of the staircase and she unwinds her legs from me, placing her feet on the stair. She steps up one, then looks down at me. "Drop your trousers."

"Don't have to tell me twice." I undo them as she stands there patiently, watching, and licks her lips ever so slightly, as she sits. With her index finger, she instructs me to come to her.

Enticing.

Alluring.

A seductive temptress.

I take one step, and with her sitting on the stair, my cock is now in her face. She lifts her hands to my hips, then moves them around and gives my ass a squeeze. I watch in fascination as her tongue darts out and licks my tip.

"At least you aren't biting it this time."

"No, I'm going to kiss it better. Would you like that?" She licks it again, just the tip, her tongue circling it.

Fuck me.

I don't think we'll make it to the bedroom if she continues that.

"Spread your legs a little wider." I do as she commands. She's in charge for now, as long as my penis stays intact, that is.

"Adora."

"Hmm," she says as she kisses my cock, her tongue working some kind of magic over him. Her hand grips my balls, and she gives them a gentle massage before I feel her fingers move farther back, but I don't say anything because her mouth takes me fully in and hits the back of her throat. Her head starts to bob and her fingers, well, her fingers go to my ass, and she pushes one in.

What the ever-loving shit?

Why the fuck does that shit feel so good?

A knock comes, and she pulls away. *Fuck that.* I reach for her and push her back onto the steps because we are far from done. But then another knock comes.

"Fuck off!" My voice is rough with lust as I hike

up her skirt. She lifts her hips, and I slide right into her. We both moan in unison.

Fucking heaven.

"I could live here," I growl.

"Let's hope not. I like to do normal things that involve taking my vagina with me," she says, leaning in and biting my shoulder.

"What the fuck? Come on, you two, we haven't even been gone long. Is that all you two know how to do?"

"Fuck off, Lucas."

"I can see your ass as you pound into your wife."

"Stop looking!" Adora tries to hide her laugh in my neck, but I thrust in deeper, making her moan again for me.

Maybe that'll shut him the fuck up.

"I mean, I would, but you're right there, your ass in the air, her legs wrapped around you. Come on, man, what are you doing? Finish already."

"Fucking hell." I tear off my shirt and throw it over Adora to cover her lower half as I pull out of her. Turning around, I find Lucas standing there, grinning. "How the fuck did you get inside?"

"What? Thought your wife might want to know her shop is on fire." Adora stands quickly, her skirt falling back into place, and she hurries up to Lucas. "Tell me you're joking."

"Not," he states casually in a complete contrast to her panic.

"I have to go." She rushes past me, and as I pass Lucas on my way after her, I smack him in the face, making him stumble backward.

"That's for ruining my day."

He laughs as Adora runs out the door.

"Yeah, yeah. You're welcome."

I swear he is a sadistic, narcissistic pig.

I pick up my shirt and walk out the front door, just catching a glimpse of Adora as she climbs into Lucas' car. She waits for me to I slide in, and as soon as the door's shut, we're driving.

"Who would want to burn down the bookstore?" she questions, breathing rapidly, her leg starting to bounce. "That place is my life. I put everything into it. I love it. It's been my refuge for so long."

"Let's wait until we get there. It might not be as bad as you think."

"Yeah, yeah, okay." I rub her leg, and she turns away from me, staring out the window the whole drive. "Well, fuck," she mumbles as it comes into view.

There are fire engines sitting out front. Even

though there are multiple firefighters with fire-fighting apparatus trying their best, it's completely gone.

There's nothing but a smoking pile of rubble left behind.

TWENTY-EIGHT

ADORA

I don't know what to do.

What do you do when the one thing you really, really love is gone?

That bookstore was my life.

I never took a day off unless I absolutely had to.

Is this payback for being away from it?

For letting someone else run it?

No, that can't be true.

Taking a week off work never killed anyone.

But it sure as shit destroyed every dream I ever had. This is my worst nightmare, and I am not sure I will recover from such a devastating blow.

Joey's hand reaches for mine, and I pull it away, not wanting his touch right now, not wanting anyone's touch right now. The officer interviews me and asks me questions, the whole time I feel numb.

My store.

Gone.

I have money, I didn't rely on this as my main income. But it was something I adored, and it was my sanctuary, my shelter from all the harm my life has thrown at me. My safe house. It's always been there for me when I've had bad days and when I have had good ones. Now what?

"Nothing is salvageable. I'm sorry," the officer tells me before he walks off. Most of the emergency services people are gone, and the bystanders who nosey into other people's misery. It's late becoming darker as we stand in front of what's left, the smell of smoke still evident in the air.

"You can open another one," Joey says, trying to comfort me. "And this time you won't need Lucas." It was Lucas' building, and his only condition was that he own a percentage of my store. I had no issue with that because Lucas had power. It was a smart move at the time to stay hidden in plain sight. However, that didn't work out as I had planned either.

Joey's hands wrap around my waist, and his mouth comes to my neck, kissing me softly.

My phone starts ringing, and I reluctantly pull it

out and answer it. I hear Sailor's voice and pull back, but Joey keeps a tight hold on me.

"I won't take no for an answer," she says. I give Joey a skeptical look, but he just leans forward and kisses my forehead.

"Sorry?" I say, confused.

"I said you aren't allowed to say no. I heard what happened, and it seems you need a night as bad as I do."

"A night?" I say confused."

"Yes. I'll pick you up in an hour. Get ready. Keir doesn't know yet, but he's watching the kids. We are going out." Then she hangs up.

I pull back and look at the phone disbelieving the words I just heard.

Joey laughs, and it pulls me out of the what-the-fuck moment I just went into.

"Keir won't allow her to be out long, or he will be monitoring her."

Right! I forget she's the wife of a mafia boss.

"What do I wear?" I ask Joey still in a state of skeptical shock.

He smacks my ass before we get into the car and head home. As soon as we arrive, I go straight into our room to change into something nicer, throw my hair up, and put on some matte lipstick. When I walk out, Joey has my black heels in his hand dangling from his finger and he's sitting on the edge of the bed. I lift a foot as he does up the strap of one and then does the same again with the second. His hand lingers on my jeans, and I wonder what he is thinking.

"Hello."

I hear the word coming from the other room as I put my foot down and walk out, not sure what to say. These feelings between us are coming at me full force.

"Oh, there you are. Good, you're ready. Let's go before he finds me." She walks up the stairs, grabs my hand, and starts pulling me. I look over my shoulder at Joey and give him a smile.

He stares at me as I leave with a sullen look on his face which instantly makes me worried.

"Does he not know you are out?" I ask.

We get into the Uber, which is waiting out front for us. I don't say anything. It's obvious if we are using an Uber that Kier knows nothing about this. Otherwise, there would be a driver and bodyguards. The thought that something could happen pops into my mind, but it's quickly gone again when Sailor starts talking.

"I snuck out. You need a hen's night. Let's pretend this is it."

"Just us two?" I ask.

"Yep, Chanel is with Lucas, and if I invite her, I know he will come." She rolls her eyes.

"Okay, so just us two." I know I am not really conversing all that well, after all, I just lost the single most important possession I have, and I am still in shock. Being dragged out for a girls' night is not something I am sure I am up for right now.

"Bingo." She smirks before she reaches for something between her breasts and pulls out a small flask opening and sculling some of the contents and then she passes it to me. "Drink up! Tonight we get wasted and then we can go back and fuck them savagely."

"Sounds like a plan." I laugh at her.

Becca slips into my mind, and I wonder again what she wanted. I need to contact her and figure it out, but right now, I try not to think about Becca and what it is she wants.

When we arrive at the club, it's packed, but Sailor skips the line and is let in.

We drink a lot.

I check the time—it's only been an hour.

We haven't stopped dancing, moving, and

drinking for that hour. And even better, Keir hasn't come to collect her. Yet.

Pulling out my phone, I text him.

Joey
Joey

I see the bubbles through blurry eyes as he messages back.

Yes, Adora.

I hate the smile on my face that he somehow always manages to pull from me.

I would very much like to fuck you right now. Maybe we can go back to the sex club and this time instead of watching me you can join in on the fun?

He types, then stops. Then types again.

Are you drunk?
Just a little.
Stay where you are, I'm coming for you.

I like it when you boss me around. Shall I
call you master as well?
Darling...
Tell me I'm your good little slut again.
Darling, I would stop saying that.
Or what?
Or I may very well bend you over my knee
and spank that ass.
Oh, I very much like the sound of that...

"I need air," I tell Sailor, sliding my phone into my pocket. The alcohol has gone to my head. I'm drunk, and I feel if I don't get air, I may very well be physically ill.

All over this dance floor.

In my pretty heels that my husband put on me.

Aww, my husband.

Maybe I will treat him to some fun.

Seems I like him after all.

"I'll be back." She only nods and keeps on dancing. I go to exit out the front door until a man in all black, who must be security, points to another door. I walk toward it and as I do, he follows opening the door.

"Thanks." I think I say it as the cold air hits me,

and then instant relief takes hold. With a deep breath, I see stairs which lead to... fuck, I got no idea. I spin back and behind me is the door back to the club which is being blocked by the security guard. "Thanks again, just needed some air." He doesn't say anything, his eyes, though, they hover on me, and even being drunk, I know I don't want his gaze. "I'll go back inside now."

"You'll do no such thing. Payment is needed for helping you, don't you think?" he asks.

"Excuse me?" I ask him, confused, clearly my drunk-addled brain has heard him wrong.

"A woman as pretty as you... all by herself is ready to be fucked." His hand touches my hair, and he lifts a strand. I knock his damn hand away, but he only laughs.

"Adora." My back stiffens when I hear *that* voice.

"Fuck off." The man in front of me says before dropping my hair.

Heavy footsteps are all I hear when I turn my head to see Joey rushing up the stairs his hands to his sides. He steps up next to me, his hand touches the side of my face while his other hand lifts, and it's followed by a loud bang.

Something wet lands on my face.

Warm and sticky.

He wipes it with his thumb.

"You really are the most beautiful thing I ever did see."

"Is that blood?" I ask him, too hypnotized by him to even care about what he just did.

I've done worse.

"Yes."

"I'm tired, I feel sick," I tell him, leaning in.

"I'll get my wife." That's Keir's voice, and then I hear the door open and close.

"Let's get you home and to my bed."

"Our bed," I say to him.

Joey's lips lift into a giant smirk.

"Yes, *ours*." He picks me up and as he carries me down the stairs, I look up to see the man dead on the steps.

Well, it sucks to be him.

That will teach him for fucking around with our family.

THE NEXT MORNING, I wake with Joey next to me. There's a book in his hands as he lays in our bed.

"Why are you so beautiful?" I ask.

He turns to look at me, putting the book down and leans in, his lips touching my bare shoulder. I briefly remember him helping me undress and putting me to bed last night.

"I need to see Becca," I tell him.

His mouth freezes against my skin, and his hands tighten on my waist.

"Can you take me?" I turn to him ever so slightly as he sucks in a breath.

"Yes." He pulls away but keeps a hand on me. "Now," is all he says followed by getting up and getting dressed.

"It can wait."

"It can't. Now, get dressed, Adora." I do because he is right. It can't wait any longer. I need to go and find out what's wrong.

The drive is quiet. For some reason, he doesn't ask me any more questions, but he should. It's probably not smart for me to go see someone I have been with, that I was falling in love with, but then again, I have been known to do stupid things in my past.

I've known them both for the same amount of time, granted I briefly knew Joey as a child, but before last week, I would have told you I knew Becca better. But as his hand grips my leg, I realize I know Joey better. He shared much with me, and I've done the same. I didn't think it was possible to fall for him, knowing our circumstances and who we are, and how much push and pull there was between us to start out.

But it's happened.

Not only is he a god at knowing my body and how it reacts, but he is hard when warranted and soft when needed.

We match perfectly.

As her apartment comes into view, his hand squeezes my leg a little tighter.

The car comes to a stop, and I reach for the door to open it, but he pulls me back, stopping me from getting out.

"Tell me you won't leave me." It's almost a plea, but he doesn't say it in that tone. He's commanding me.

"I'll be back. I don't know how long this will take, but I'll be back."

"You'll be back," he repeats, nods, and lets me go. "I'll wait here." I get out of the car and walk up the stairs to her door. I knock a few times, but she doesn't answer. So, I knock again. When the door finally opens, it's not her standing there, it's a lady dressed in scrubs.

"Hi, can I help you?"

"Oh, sorry, yeah... I'm here to see Becca. This is her place, correct?"

"It is. I've just given her some medication, but you can come in now before she goes to sleep. She was still awake when I left her."

"Medicine? Is she sick?"

Her mouth draws into a tight line. "I think it's best you ask her that. You are her visitor."

"How long have you worked for her?"

"A few months now." She holds the door open. "You must be Adora. I've heard wonderful things about you."

"Thank you." Looking over my shoulder to Joey, who's still in the car, then back to the woman. "Can I see her?"

"Of course. Go on in." She holds the door open for me and shuts it after I enter. "To the right." Walking farther in, I see the end of a bed covered in pink sheets and a pair of bare legs resting on top of the covers. My eyes move up to find Becca curled up in a ball with her back to me.

"Becca." Her body stiffens at the sound of my voice. She slowly turns her head toward me. "Are you okay?" I ask, stepping farther into her room. "You left in a rush."

"I wanted to tell you, not for you to find out like this." She manages to sit up. When she's situated, she reaches for the water next to her bed, which sits on a small table littered with multiple bottles of pills and other paraphernalia. Her hands are shaky, so I step forward and grab it for her.

"Here." I hand her the cup and she puts it to her lips. It's then I see her cheeks are sunken in and there are dark shadows under her eyes.

"Thank you." Her voice is weak, and she takes some more water, then pulls the cup away and places it back on the bedside table.

"Are you sick?" I ask, feeling more terrified by the second.

She manages to give me a small smile. "A tumor. I found out the day I came to your bookstore the first time. I remember seeing you and thinking, *'I normally wouldn't say anything to this beautiful lady, but today I got bad news, and I plan to turn that around.'*" She blinks her eyes a few times. "I have good days and bad days. Right now is bad. So excuse me I need to sit back." She rests against the back of the bed, leaning on it.

"And all this will help?"

"No, nothing will help." Her words shock me, and I feel my chest constrict.

"What do you mean?" I ask, not believing her.

"I'm dying. The doctor says it will be sooner

rather than later." She shrugs. "The bad days are starting to outweigh the good ones."

"I'm..." Words don't want to leave me, but I manage some anyway. "Is this why you've been trying to reach me?"

She touches her head, and I can see she's lost weight. *How did I not see that before?*

"Yes, I planned to tell you. Then you broke it off, and I figured it was better you didn't know. Then I told my parents." Tears drip from her eyes and run down her cheeks. She wipes at them angrily, then she lets out a humorless laugh. "They said this happened to me because of who I chose to love... that it's not normal."

I take two steps and wrap my arms around her, hugging her to me. She starts to cry even harder, and I feel so lost, broken for her. How can parents let alone anyone be that cruel? Becca is not a bad person. She is probably the nicest person I know—caring and loving—and to top it off, they raised her, so no matter what, they should love her.

Isn't that what a good parent is meant to do?

My father was a crap parent, but I knew where I stood with him.

Becca, she had hope.

And they crushed it.

And so did I.

"Are you happy with him?" she asks softly.

"I think I could be, yes." I pull back to see her watching me as she wipes her tears away. "He already loves you. I can see it in his eyes. You're an easy woman to love."

"I don't think we're there just yet," I tell her honestly, but she shakes her head slightly.

"It's amazing how fast love swoops in and saves you, makes you feel things you've never felt before and gives you a new sense of life." Her hands clutch her head, and I back up, afraid I may hurt her. "Sorry, the dizzy spells get me."

"Do they happen often?" I ask, concerned.

"More so lately."

"And there's absolutely no treatment?"

"They offered, but I refused. It's so far advanced already that it would just make me more uncomfortable. I don't want to go through all that when I know the outcome."

"Why didn't you tell me sooner?" I ask.

"You had so much going on already. You were marrying a man in the mafia. That within itself can be a death sentence." She manages to throw a smile my way.

"Can I continue to visit?"

"I want to thank you, Adora..." She lies back down fully on her bed, pulling the covers up as I stand next to her.

"For what?"

"For giving me something I knew I always wanted. To love someone." I wipe the tears from my cheeks that are now free-falling.

"Adora."

We both turn in the direction of the door to see Joey standing there.

"I'm not ready," I say to him, still wiping at my face.

"I spoke to your nurse," Joey says to Becca, his focus on her frail body curled up in her bed.

"I didn't mean to ruin your honeymoon. I'm truly sorry," Becca replies, her eyes holding sadness and now exhaustion. I sit on the edge of her bed and clutch her hand in mine. She offers me a knowing look, then glances at Joey. "Do you know how lucky you are?"

"I do," Joey says without missing a beat, and if my heart wasn't broken it would be beating for him.

"You'll treat her right?" Becca asks.

"With everything I am."

"Why do I believe you?" Becca lets out a huff of

a laugh. "I guess you know how to kill someone easily so she will be protected."

I manage a small laugh too.

Joey steps farther into the room, and his hand comes to rest on my shoulder. "I would like to offer you something if you would be willing?" We both glance at him. His ice-blue eyes flick to mine before they land on Becca. "No one should die alone. We have a room, good doctors, and your nurse can come too."

Becca and I sit there, both of us taken aback at his more than generous offer.

I didn't expect him to say that.

Not at all.

"I slept with your wife," Becca states simply. My eyes go wide, and I bite my lip at her words. "You want to share a house with someone who also loves your wife?"

"Yes, because while you had her for a short while, I will have her for a lifetime."

Ouch, that was mean.

"I want to say no," Becca replies, but then she glances at me. "But I'm also afraid. I don't want to die alone." She looks at me pleadingly. "Would you want me there?"

Taking a deep breath, I look back at Joey. His

eyes are already on me, waiting for me to answer. He's given me his approval, so it's down to me.

"You're okay with it if I say yes?"

He lifts my chin ever so slightly. "You are all I see, and if this will make you happy, then, yes, I'm okay with it."

My free hand reaches up and captures his. He gives it a kiss before quickly releasing it.

Looking back to Becca, I ask, "What do you need me to pack?"

TWENTY-NINE

JOEY

It's not ideal, the situation I've created. I won't lie and say it's easy. Becca's been living here now for a week. And for the whole week I've hardly seen my wife, or slept in the same bed as my wife, or even fucked my wife.

I hear her laugh when I get home, hear her soft voice in the mornings when I leave.

I can't blame her—I did agree to this.

Hell, it was my idea.

It felt like the right thing to do, to show Adora my trust in her. Make her trust me. It's what our relationship is missing.

"I didn't take you for much of a cook." Adora's hands circle my waist as she comes up behind me and leans her head on my back as she breathes me in.

"I can cook a mean bacon and eggs."

She giggles into my shoulder. "If you were taught by your mother, I absolutely believe you."

"No, my last girlfriend," I joke, but she freezes behind me. "Adora." I turn around and her hands drop to her sides. "I'm kidding." I push her long chocolate hair behind her ears and lift her face to look at me. Those eyes that are full of bottomless whiskey stare back at me tiredly.

"If I say something, do you swear to not lose your shit?"

"If you promise to sleep in our bed tonight."

"I do."

"So do I, then," I tell her, my hands trailing across her shoulders and down her arms.

"It's hard to give you my all when a part of me is in that back room." She doesn't look where Becca is currently sleeping, but we both know that's who she's referring to.

"For someone who grew up without love, you sure do have enough of it to give," I say evenly, keeping my anger at bay. It's not necessary. I understand what she's saying, as much as it might frustrate me.

"We haven't shared those words," she points out,

nibbling on her lip. "I don't intend to any time soon, just so you're aware."

"And why is that?"

"Do you love me?" she questions, her eyes never leaving mine. "You're falling for me, I can tell that much, and I'm falling for you too. But love isn't instant. It may be fast when it hits you, but it takes time to get to that point. I could have fallen deeply in love with Becca if you hadn't come along."

"I am falling for you." Might be a bit of an understatement right now, but I am not going to lay everything on the line.

"And I am for you, but you must know I'm not there yet, Joey. I can put up a shield as fast as you can say *happy*. I've done it before, and I will probably do it again. I'm trying to be more..." she thinks on the word, "... *me* here, and not the me that was broken back home."

"Do you want to stay in our bedroom tonight?" I ask, and she falls into my chest.

"Yes, it's been a week, and I miss you terribly." Her answer settles me in a way I didn't realize I needed, so I wrap my arms around her. "Never thought I'd say that considering where we started." I stroke her hair and kiss it, taking in her beautiful scent.

"Sometimes the rockiest of starts can lead to the best outcomes." The bacon starts sizzling, and I pull her with me as I turn around to flip it.

"I'm going to shower. Do you think you can take Becca some food? See if she'll eat?"

I grip Adora's face between my hands and kiss her lips, and her hands cover mine as she kisses me back with tenderness. Her body pushes up against mine, and our mouths open at the exact same time as our tongues start to dance.

I could kiss her for a lifetime.

And every lifetime after that.

She tastes like peppermint and simply... her.

She pulls away first, and I lean in and kiss her lips one more time. "Go, I'll join you after." I smack her ass before I turn back to the stove, making her smile as she shakes her head before walking off. After finishing up the food, I take a plate to the room where Becca is staying. It used to be an office, but we easily turned it into a bedroom for her. I was able to get all the medical equipment in quickly, and she is comfortable in the right type of bed that she needs.

Becca is sitting up in her adjustable bed and watching the television when I walk in.

"Adora insisted you eat," I tell her, grabbing the tray and placing it over her lap. It's a simple meal, just a few pieces of bacon, a slice of toast, and an egg. Adora has said she doesn't eat all that much. I guess that's what happens when you reach the end of life —*what is food to you then?*

"Can I ask you something?" She looks down at the food, not bothering to touch it.

"If you eat a piece of bacon, you can ask me whatever."

"Anything?" I give her a nod, and she lifts the smallest piece and puts it to her lips, taking a bite. I watch as she struggles with just that tiny bit. When she's done, she reaches for the glass of water, taking a sip before looking back at me. "How many people have you killed?"

"Why? Do you plan to report me to the authorities?" I joke with her. She shakes her head. "Well into the hundreds. Why?"

"Do you feel like your hands are tainted when you touch her?"

"No," I answer truthfully. "We learn early on to not feel guilt and certainly not to focus on what needs to be done. Would it make you feel better if I said I felt guilty?"

"No, I just want to understand you better, I guess. See what type of man you really are."

"For what? Your approval? You do realize I don't

need it. She's my wife." Her eyes blink a few times, and she looks back down at her food, lifting another piece of bacon to her lips and taking a small bite before she puts it back down. "You do know she's no angel, correct?"

"I know. But behind her tough exterior is a very caring person. She could have kept fighting this... whatever it is you two have... but she gave in. Are you not glad she did?"

"I am."

"So what I'm saying is... that I see her differently than you do. We probably love her for similar reasons, though."

"I don't love her. It's too soon."

"How soon is too soon to love someone?" She raises a brow. "I don't know the exact number of days I have left, but I know they aren't many. What do you plan to do to help her when I'm gone?" When I don't answer, she carries on, "She has a secret, did you know?"

"We all have secrets," I tell her, even though now I'm eager to know what secret she's talking about and what Adora is keeping from me.

"She has one that she only just recently shared with me. When I asked her if she had told you, she replied with *'he isn't ready to hear that just yet.'*" She shrugs, and my eyes narrow as I digest that comment. "Maybe you aren't, maybe you are, but you have to prove to her you are at least willing to try."

"I am trying."

"Are you?" She yawns and lies back in the bed, so I remove the plate and tray. "I see what she sees in you, Joey. I see it."

I don't ask her what she means.

Her eyes close, and she falls asleep.

Becca's phone starts buzzing on the bedside table. I ignore it until it goes off again, so I walk back to wake her, but decide against it. When I glance at the phone's screen, I see it's her mother calling, and I answer it.

"Hello."

"Oh, sorry. Is this Becca's phone?" An older voice comes through the line.

"It is..." I pause. "She's sleeping."

"Okay, well, I was hoping I could visit her, but she no longer lives in her apartment. You wouldn't happen to know where she might be?" I look down at her sleeping form. If I were dying, I would want to see my mother, so I give her the address, and she tells me she'll be over in a few hours. Putting the phone back down, I grab the plate and take it to the kitchen before I go upstairs to find Adora. She's standing at the window, a towel wrapped around her, just staring outside.

"Adora."

She turns, her back against the windowsill, and drops her towel. Her hands fall to her sides, and her eyes, dark with need, lock on mine. "I need to feel something other than..." I know what she's asking before I even get to her. I lift her, and her arms wrap around my neck, her legs circling my waist. She looks down at me tenderly, pushing a strand of hair away from my face. "I'm glad we found each other, Joey."

I kiss her, and she kisses me back with a force so strong that if her back wasn't already against the window, we may have fallen.

It's in this moment I know without a doubt that she will consume me, wholly.

THIRTY

ADORA

Warm hands caress each and every part of my body, making me feel something other than sadness. I crave it. He craves it.

Joey is by far the best lover I have ever been with.

He seems to know exactly where to touch and when. It's as if he can read my mind.

It's funny when I think about our beginning, which in reality wasn't all that long ago, but for some reason, it feels like I've known him a lifetime.

Yes, I may be holding back a secret from him—one I'm not entirely sure how to tell him—but it's not because I don't care for him. I simply have to find the right time.

His jeans have dropped to the floor, and I can

feel him exactly where I need him. He groans when I sink onto him, and I let a moan slip free from my lips.

"Tell me," he demands.

I don't know what he's asking, but I have a fair idea.

He pulls my head back so he can see my face. "Tell me, Adora. Tell me no other can fuck you the way I can. Tell me!" He basically growls out the words.

I ignore him for a second until he's seated so deep, I can feel him everywhere.

"Well, you aren't fucking me right now," I say back to him as I feel myself clench around him.

"Tell me," he says it again. "I can feel your pussy, Adora. It loves my cock. Do you love my cock?"

"Very much so." I run my fingers over his lips and goosebumps rise in their wake. "I also like what these can do to my pussy." He moves quickly, my hair swinging as he does, and places me on the floor. He pulls out of me and slides down my body until I feel his warm breath between my thighs.

His mouth kisses my mound before his tongue darts out and licks my clit. Warmth spreads through me as I reach down and lace my hands through his hair. He grunts, the vibration from the sound making me whimper before he slips a digit inside me and fucks me with both his mouth and fingers.

I clutch my breast and pinch my nipple as I feel the orgasm building higher and higher with every flick of his tongue and suction of his lips. He continues his movements, never once slowing or changing tempo, knowing that the pace he is at right now is exactly what is needed.

"Now you tell me," I yell at him, and he chuckles. Then, as I come, he pulls his fingers away and his warmth is gone, immediately missed. When I open my eyes, I see him crawling up my body, his mouth arriving at my nipples, taking one in his mouth and letting it pop out before he does the same with the other.

"Tell you what, darling?"

"Tell me I'm your favorite."

He sits on his knees, his cock hard and ready, his shirt lost in the process, a possessive look plastered all over his face. His hands come to my knees, and he holds them down, spreading them wider. He leans down and kisses the inside of my knee, then kisses his way up until he gets to my sensitive pussy. He gives it a slow lick, then slides a finger in and pulls it out before putting it into his mouth. After the digit is sucked clean, he licks his lips and continues his torture, every touch eliciting a needy moan from my throat. He leaves a trail of kisses all the way up my stomach, then bites my nipples, making me yelp in surprise. I'm watching him with eager eyes as we come face to face.

"There will never be another you, nor has there ever been. You have no competition."

"You said I wasn't your type," I point out breathily.

"You weren't. But now you are the only type I see." My heart swells as he leans down and continues to kiss me. He finally slides into me, and our mouths connect, and soon we are rocking into oblivion.

Lips, tongues, us—all one.

He goes slowly, tenderly.

And he does just what I asked him to do.

He makes me forget.

Until all I can see and hear is him.

***

"SOMEONE IS HERE." My head lifts from his chest. His hand is stroking my hair, and I'm almost asleep. I get up and go to the closet to grab a new set of clothes, and when I walk out, Joey is already fully dressed.

"It's Becca's mother."

My eyes go wide at his words.

"What? How would you know that?" I ask as I pass him on my way to the stairs.

"She rang Becca's phone when I was down there, and I answered. She was looking for her, so I told her she was here."

I pause at the top of the stairs. "You had no right to do that."

He reaches for me, and I pull away, turning to face him. "You had no right. They didn't care that she was dying. They don't care about her at all."

"I think that's the reason she's here. She cares now," he states, but he doesn't know the whole story. I shake my head and continue down the stairs until I reach the door. Pulling it open, I find a lady standing there, her bag clutched to her side. I know straight away she's Becca's mother. They look alike with the same blonde hair and bone structure. Her eyes take me in, then move to Joey behind me.

"Hi, I'm Samantha, Becca's mother. We spoke on the phone."

Joey steps up next to me and offers her his hand. She shakes it and places hers back to her side.

"I'll see if she's awake." Joey heads off while Samantha studies me.

"This is a lovely home. Have you known my daughter for long?" she asks, probably expecting an introduction I'm not willing to give her.

"Not all that long."

"That's super helpful of him to offer her a place to stay."

"It's what a good person would do, wouldn't you say?" I reply pointedly as Joey returns.

"I have to speak to Joey for a second, do you mind?"

Samantha nods, and Joey shuts the door, looking confused. When it's closed behind us, I look up at him expectantly.

"Becca wants to ask us something, what did you need to ask me?" he says.

"Nothing." I shake my head needing to step away from that woman. I spin on my heel and head for Becca's room. She's picking nervously at her nails when I walk in, and she wastes no time before she speaks, "Joey, will you say you're my boyfriend?" I look back over my shoulder to find Joey behind me.

"This won't bother you?" he asks me.

One of my legs starts shaking, and I find it hard to stand still.

"She doesn't want conflict with her mother since she took the step to visit her," I manage to say, but I look back at Becca. "You should tell her. You don't want to lie to her."

"But I do. She hates me for what I am. This way, she won't. This way I will go to the grave, and she will think no less of me."

"You're amazing just as you are," I add, hating that she thinks she has to do this. That her mother, of all people, would make her feel like this. That she has to hide who she is, that she has to feel that insecure in her own life.

"If you hadn't fucked my wife, I may even like you," Joey adds, and she cracks a smile. "I'll do it. Of course, I will. I'll bring her in now."

"Thank you, Joey," Becca whispers as Joey walks away.

"I'm sorry. I didn't know what else to do." Her eyes glance to the door.

"It's fine. It will be fine," I say to reassure us both. I step around to the other side of the bed. Slipping my hand under the covers, I grab her fingers and give them a tight squeeze. She hasn't seen her mother for such a long time—her parents wanting nothing to do with her when she came out.

"Becca."

Becca turns away from me, her hand leaving

mine as she looks at her mother standing in the doorway.

"I..."

"We should leave," Joey says to me, and I look at him in shock.

We should *not* leave.

We don't know what type of woman she is.

We don't know how she is going to treat her.

How can we leave Becca alone with her?

"If you don't mind," Samantha says, reaching out and touching Joey's arm. "Thank you."

Joey reaches for me, but I pull away and walk straight to the kitchen and start pacing.

"You need to calm down."

I spin to face him. "I was calm until you took a call from someone who didn't even care her child is dying," I basically scream at him.

He steps up to me, his hands gliding along my arms to try to soothe me, and it almost works until I see Becca's door opening and her mother stepping out.

I pull away from Joey and walk straight over to her. "Is she okay?" I look past her to see Becca struggling to keep her eyes open. "She gets tired easily," I explain.

"Mom." We all turn to see Becca looking at us. "Is Dad coming?"

Samantha shakes her head and wipes away a stray tear that is falling down her cheek.

Becca nods and closes her eyes again.

"It's kind of you to love her. Thank you." She steps up to Joey and hugs him. "Her father will be happy to know she didn't die with her soul sinning."

For fuck's sake! I ball up my fists and barely avoid hitting her.

"Will you be coming back?" Joey asks, distracting her from looking at me.

"No, I said my goodbye. She knows I love her, even though I didn't approve of her choices recently."

"You don't want to be here when she passes away?" I blurt out, not believing a mother could not possibly want to be with their child at a time like this regardless of whether they have met their expectations in life.

Joey's eyes find mine, and he shakes his head infinitesimally.

"I am here. And she has days, maybe only hours. She told you I was a doctor, right?" She turns back to me to direct that question.

"No, she did not."

"She's tired, can barely hold a conversation. I've seen many patients at the end of life. She chose not to do any treatment, and I respect that. Sometimes not all treatments are good for you and can make you sicker, therefore, your quality of life deteriorates. Her pain is managed, but she is nearing the end. She doesn't have long."

"And you can just leave?" I ask her incredulously.

"I can. Thank you both again." She makes her way to the door and walks out. I'm left standing there angry, so incredibly angry at a mother who can be like that. Someone who raised you, loved you, but didn't want anything to do with you because of who you loved. At least mine is just gone, and I don't have many memories of her. And those I do are fleeting and not all that great.

"Your mother would never do that to you or Keir," I say to Joey, a tear escaping as I look up at him. He manages to laugh, but it's humorless as he swipes a thumb across my cheek and pulls me to him.

"No, she wouldn't." He kisses the top of my head and gently rocks me from side to side. "Adora."

"Hmm."

We hear something fall, and I'm moving fast

before I can even think twice. I find Becca on her side, her eyes open, and her phone on the floor.

"Joey!" I scream.

He comes in, pushes past me, and immediately lays her down and starts doing CPR. I stand at the door, unsure of what to do. It feels like I'm frozen to the spot, my heart beating so fast I can't think straight.

His eyes flick back to me. "Call my doctor," he demands. "Adora," he says it louder, snapping me back into action, and nods to his phone in his back pocket. I reach for it and do as he asks, dismissing the picture of me on his screen sucking his cock. The doctor answers straight away and tells us he's on his way.

Joey never stops CPR.

Not even when the doctor arrives.

Not even when the doctor says there is nothing else he can do.

Not even as I fall to the floor, unable to hold myself up a second longer.

Then she is pronounced dead.

How can this be possible?

How can someone just... die?

That's not fair.

This is not fair.

My hands bang on Joey's chest as I scream at him, sobbing and trembling. He picks me up and carries me out, my tears soaking his shirt, and I can't even fathom looking to see where he takes me.

He places me on a bed then scoots in behind me, and I know it's ours straightaway, the feel of it evident in the sheets, and his smell is everywhere.

I hear a knock on the door, and Joey's soft voice follows. "Clean it all up, keep the valuables."

I know in my head what he's talking about, but my brain doesn't seem to want to compute that he's referring to Becca's things.

I was only talking to her earlier, and now...

How can that happen so quickly?

I don't get it.

I don't.

I didn't get to say my goodbye.

And my heart just won't stop breaking, splitting inside my chest. It cracks, then cracks some more.

How is this healthy?

Can you die of a broken heart?

Because I feel like at any moment, I just might.

THIRTY-ONE

JOEY

On and off for hours straight, I wipe her tears away until I think Adora can't cry anymore, then she cries again.

I don't know how to help her other than being here for her. My job is to kill people, so death and I are old friends.

This feels weird, but also right that I'm here for her.

She ends up falling asleep in my arms eventually, and I stay like that until the next morning when I wake and don't find her with me.

Walking down the stairs, I find her sitting on the bottom step, her head hanging between her legs.

"I need my bubble," she hiccups between tears.

I lift her to her feet, grab my phone and blast

some music, and wrap her arms around my neck as I start to slow dance with her. Our hips are rocking, and her head is resting against my chest.

"Darling."

"I like it when you call me that. Even without the emphasis from when you were so mad at me you couldn't think straight."

We continue to rock back and forth.

"I like calling you darling," I tell her, kissing the top of her head.

"You got rid of all her things. It doesn't even look like she was here, even though I can still smell her in there."

"There is a box of her things on the counter," I tell her, my hands smoothing up her back to try and calm her breathing. She tries to pull away, but I tug her back. "You need the bubble a little longer." She looks up at me with those whiskey eyes and drinks me in. The look she's giving me makes her even more beautiful, as torn apart as she is.

"I wish I hated you," she says softly. "But I'm glad I don't." When she pulls away this time, I let her go. Following her, I see her opening the box and pulling out Becca's phone, a photograph of her, and another small box. She glances back at me. "Do you know what this is?" I nod my head.

The box has Adora's name on it. When she opens it, she sucks in a breath—it's pages torn from books, with highlighted words.

"To the one who helped me breathe again." She reads it out loud, then continues, *"I was lost, before I was found. I was broken, before you put me back together. How can one person manage to have such a large impact in such a small amount of time?"* She glances back at me. "This must have taken her ages." She pauses, glancing up at me. When I don't answer, she asks, "Did you know?"

I give her a simple nod.

"Did you help?"

Another nod. I don't intend to lie to my wife.

"I'm not sure if I'm upset about the books being torn or that she isn't here for me to tell her I'm upset."

"I sourced the books from book bins. They were being recycled anyway." She sighs, her lips trembling with a fresh wave of tears. "I knew you would hate for me to tear up perfectly good books."

Taking a shaky breath, her eyes search mine as she gives me a small nod before she turns back and continues to go through the pages. I pour her a glass of water as she sits down on the floor, laying the pages out in front of her.

"I need to go to Keir. But I will stay if you need me."

"No, I want time with this. Thank you." Reaching up for me, I lean down, and she presses a light kiss to my lips. When I look at her face, she's smiling, but it's a sad one. One that has me wishing I could stay.

I head to the door and order food to be delivered in the next hour to make sure she eats before I walk out.

"Joey." Her voice halts me at the door. "I am very close to saying I love you. But you don't deserve those words when I'm full of pain."

"That's fine, Adora, I can wait. I've waited this long. What's a little while longer?" I tell her before I leave, contentment filling my chest to hear those words from her.

I'll wait as long as she needs me to.

"YOU'VE GONE HOME to check on her twice already. She is fine. Enough," Lucas says, shaking his head.

"She's my wife."

"Whoop dee do," Lucas says. "Keir has a wife, and you don't see him running home every second."

"Can we kill him?" I ask Keir, but he doesn't even pay us any attention.

Piper, on the other hand, nods her head. Piper is trusted as much as Lucas, maybe even more since he defied Keir's orders a while ago. She enjoys what we do, and no other woman has held such a strong position as she does. I would like to think it's because of who Keir is married to. He was meant to have a son to take over from him, but he had a girl first. And Sailor argued with him that a woman can be just as badass as any man. And it worked.

"I should shoot you again. Why are you even here?" Lucas says to her. Piper pulls her gun out, and he just cracks a taunting smile, not even fazed that she has it aimed at his damn boof head. She's a good shot too, she will not miss if given half a chance.

"Put your lady bits away." Lucas waves a hand at her. "Unless you want me to get the big boy out?" Lucas looks down to his crotch, but we all know that's not what he's referring to. He's most definitely talking about his Smith and Wesson 500 handgun that's tucked into his pants.

"You are all types of fucked-up. How Chanel

hasn't managed to slit your throat when you're sleeping is beyond me."

"I'm just too charming." Lucas shrugs smugly.

"Enough," Keir growls as the man we've been waiting for exits the club. The minute he sees us, his eyes go wide, and his hands slide into his pockets.

"Guys." He nods, stepping over to us.

Lucas pushes off the car and walks over to him, pacing around him like a cat, and stops at his back. "Birdies have been telling me stories, Brian."

Brian tries to stay very calm, very still.

"You remember who we are, right?" I ask him.

Brian nods his head in quick, successive jerks.

Jake, who owns the sex club, gave me a heads-up when Brian arrived.

"Of course."

"And you know we have multiple businesses?" I ask him, casually leaning against the car as Piper and Keir stay quiet.

"For example, I co-owned a little bookstore," Lucas states.

We watch him closely. His brows pinch together, his face tightens, and beads of sweat build on his face as he tries to hold his expression still to not give anything away.

It isn't working.

"I mean, you know anything I own is well protected, right? With security cameras and the whole works," Lucas says, leaning in and whispering into Brian's ear.

Brian's face starts to go red.

"Are we the type of people you want to anger, Brian?" I question with a bit of a bite.

Jake walks out, a cigarette to his lips and a lighter in one hand. He gives us all a nod before he turns around to head back inside.

"Jake, please don't leave me out here with them."

Jake doesn't stop. While Jake may be a terrifying man in his own right, he knows better. We have respect from Jake, but Brian seems to have forgotten what respect is.

"Guys, please. They made me."

"They made you?" Piper says, then throws her head back and laughs. "I checked your bank account and saw you got paid for your *little job*." She steps straight up to him and reaches inside his jeans pocket and pulls out his phone. Turning it to face him, she unlocks it with the face ID and steps back next to Keir. "He really needs to learn to use the delete button," Piper mutters with a smile before she shows Keir. "Look at his location." Keir looks up at me. "Italy." Piper gets in the car where her computer is located and takes his phone with him.

I hold the back door open and wave to Brian. "Come on, Brian, it's time we go for a little drive."

"No, please, I don't want to," Brian cries.

Lucas kicks the back of his legs so he falls forward, and barely manages to catch himself with his hands before doing a face-plant on the concrete. "Please, I'm begging you."

"I would get in the car, *now*," I say to him.

Lucas walks around to the other side as Brian gets up and into the car. He crawls into the middle, and I sit on his other side. Keir drives the car with Piper in the passenger seat on her computer.

"They didn't even pay that well," she says, shaking her head. "I mean, if you're going to commit a felony, at least make an exceptional amount of money out of it. This is more of a payment for robbing grandma's house."

"Please don't kill me." Brian starts crying, and it's embarrassing.

"That's up to Lucas. You did burn down his building," I tell him, lifting my brows.

Everyone knows not to grovel to Lucas because it never works. But, Brian, I've got to give it to him, he tries anyway.

"Lucas, please. Please, I'll help rebuild. They didn't say it was yours, just that I needed to teach the bitch a lesson."

"Bitch?" Lucas asks.

Reaching into my pocket, I pull out the cable ties I planned to use on him later.

"Yes, some whore he wanted to let know he was coming for."

I don't think clearly, at least that's my excuse, as I lift the cable ties and put them around his neck and squeeze. Lucas just sits there watching while Brian struggles to pull free. I hold still as Brian's elbows knock into my stomach and his hands go to my jeans and try to dig in.

"Probably shouldn't have called his wife a whore," Lucas says, smiling, and finally reaches for Brian's hands, holding them down as I pull a little tighter. "He's a real cunt when mad, and now I have to deal with him. Thanks, Brian," Lucas adds with an eye roll. "You can die now."

Keir pulls down a dark alley as I feel Brian's struggle weaken, and when we get to a stop, I pull his lifeless body from the car and throw him in the river.

Where he belongs.

Only I can call my wife a whore.

My little whore, to be precise.

Adora

It's been a week since Becca passed away, and her ashes sit in our house in a beautiful vase. Her parents didn't want them. I'm not sure what to do with them or where to put them, but I'm sure that will come with time.

Joey has been... nothing short of amazing. He's working a lot. But he always makes time to come check in on me. It took me days to go through all the pages Becca left for me because tears would clog my eyes, and I couldn't go further. But today I didn't wake up and start crying, so I guess that is progress.

I'm used to not waking up with Joey now. I took me a while, but finally, I know he will be all right and he always comes home. In the morning, he heads for work before I get up and kisses me every morning before he leaves. I feel it on my cheek as he lingers, and I promptly go back to sleep.

Walking down the stairs, I hear soft music. It's Sunday and, even though he usually works all the time, he told me he was going to have the day off to spend some time with me.

His voice echoes through the downstairs area as he sings. He has a lovely voice, one I could listen to for days. I follow the sound and stop just inside the door. He looks up from his spot on the floor and studies me for a reaction—I've had so many emotional reactions this week I am not surprised he needs to check to make sure I am okay. He brought me dessert home one night, and I put it straight in the sink and walked off. Another night he came home, and I ran into his arms and couldn't seem to let go. So he carried me awkwardly up the stairs to our bed and laid me on his chest, and that's how I fell asleep.

Ups and downs.

But I'm ready for the normal now.

If that's even possible.

Yesterday he sent Troy to stay with me all day, and that helped more than I care to admit. Sometimes all a girl needs is her best friend. They just get you, help you.

"You built me this?" I ask in awe. I told him I wanted to change it, and he completely changed it, and now it's covered in books. "Where did the books come from?"

"I bought them all."

I'm too stunned to speak. He remembered from when I first came to his home that I wanted to change the bookshelf area and make it more... *mine*. He did everything I said. It's full of romance, fantasy, and paranormal books—every single one of them are my favorites, but he also has an all-time favorite area.

Stepping up to them, I run my hand along every spine.

"How did you have the time?" I ask as he sorts through the bottom shelf.

"I painted it when you fell asleep, and I've been up for a few hours adding the books," he says simply. I look down at him, shaking my head at how incredibly thoughtful and sweet this whole thing is and how he's acting like it's no big deal.

It is a big deal.

It's a major act of kindness, and I will never forget how he caters to my wishes.

"My badass husband is sitting on the floor, holding romance books in his hands instead of a gun to make me happy?" I offer him a smile that's quickly taking over my face.

He gives me an eye roll in return. "Would it be more macho if I went out on the street, shot someone, and came back with blood on my hands? A man's gotta do what a man's got to do."

I shrug my shoulders. "I mean if that's what floats your boat." He reaches for me and pulls me down to him, my ass landing on his lap. He pushes my hair back behind my ear and kisses me tenderly on my neck. "Thank you," I tell him, feeling myself melting into his hold.

"What for?"

"Everything."

"It's what a husband and wife do. We don't keep secrets and we help each other when we need to."

"No secrets," I repeat, nodding my head.

"Do you have any secrets?" he asks, leaving another kiss on my jaw.

I turn on his lap and wrap my legs around him, and I feel him getting hard. "Secrets," I whisper, more to myself.

"Yes, I hate liars. So don't lie to me, Adora." As he says it, he pulls my hips in closer, and I feel him between my legs. I only have on one of his shirts, nothing else, while he's in a pair of boxers. My arms wrap around him, and my nails scrape down his back as I start to grind my hips down on him. I can feel myself getting wet and know full well his boxers aren't going to be clean after this.

We haven't had sex all week.

He's touched me, yes, but nothing sexual. He's let me be, only providing comfort when I need it.

But right now, I want him.

Secrets.

Sometimes a girl needs her secrets.

No one should know everything about someone else.

It's not right.

Is it?

Then again, I've never seen a healthy relationship in my life.

Is what Joey and I have healthy? I would say probably not, but it's not terrible either.

He cares for me, more than anyone. His small gestures, hell, even his large gestures—hello... bookcase—are proof positive.

But again, we all need secrets.

And not everything should be shared.

"Fuck, you are so beautiful." I believe every word he's saying like it's the air he breathes. He eagerly reaches between us and pulls himself free, then inserts himself into me in one smooth motion, and we both share a groan of relief. "Your pussy was made for me."

And I believe it was. No other has made me feel this way. Made me feel this good. It's like my body was sculpted, especially for him.

Even if I wasn't originally his type.

"The people I would kill to keep them from having the pleasure of watching you come. No one will ever see what's mine." He slaps my ass as my hips move up and down. "Will they, my darling little wife? You are all *mine*."

I whimper, which only makes him slap me again, harder.

"Tell me, wife. Tell me how much you like it when my cock is in you, that your sweet pussy craves only what it can give." He leans in and whispers, "That you only crave my cock. Tell me now."

"Fuck, yes, all of it. Only you."

"Good wifey." His hand snakes up my chest and pinches my nipple before he reaches my throat. He pushes me back, my hands behind me, so my breasts are pushed up in the air as I continue riding his cock. His other hand goes to his mouth before he sucks his finger, then presses it to my lips. "Open." I do as he says, and he puts two fingers in my mouth. "Suck." Again, I do as he asks. "Now spit." I spit on his fingers, and he pulls them away before he reaches between us and presses them to my clit and starts rubbing in slow, deliberate circles.

Circles of heaven.

That's the only way to describe them.

"Faster, now." His voice is low, hard, and all but demanding. I move my hips faster while he maintains pressure on my throat with one hand, and the other continues rubbing my clit.

"Joey." His name leaves my lips like a plea.

"Yes, wife."

"Fuck..."

"I'm already doing that, darling. Now, unless you plan to bounce on my cock, I would shut up and let me fuck you."

The way he talks to me, fucks me, it's the perfect mix of everything.

I found a happy place.

And it's right here.

In the arms of this man.

COSTUME PARTY IS the theme tonight for Chanel's birthday. I asked Joey yesterday what his favorite character was, and he smirked and said he always wanted his own Playboy bunny. So that's exactly what I have done. I hired the costume and now I'm walking down the stairs while he waits at the bottom for me.

"You aren't dressed?" I ask him when his eyes find mine.

He's dressed in a suit.

"I am."

"Not in character."

"I'm always in character," he says as I get closer. When I reach him, he takes my hand and slowly spins me in a circle. After I've done a full spin and face him once again, his eyes are hungry, and he's biting his bottom lip. "We can stay in."

"I need to get out. Besides, it's Chanel's birthday, and I like her."

"Well, I plan to fuck you either way, so I'd stay close." I laugh as I step past him, and he smacks my ass. The driver is already waiting out front for us, and we climb into the car. Joey's eyes stay on me for the whole drive. I'm wearing a curly blonde wig and the bunny ears, and a small little suit with black stockings and pink heels.

His eyes don't leave me.

"Lose the hair." He nods to it.

I touch it, smiling.

"He always had a thing for blondes, so I figured I would dress the part."

"Lose the wig. I don't have a thing for blondes, I have a thing for sassy little chocolate brunettes who can't get enough of my cock." He reaches forward and grabs the ears as I pull the wig off and let my hair fall free, then he puts the ears back on me. "There, now it's perfect." He grabs my boob, and I give him a strange look. "Just getting in my feels before we have to get out." That makes me laugh.

"So you don't plan to touch me again once we're out of the car?" I pout.

"I plan to fuck you the minute I can, but it's a bit hard with eyes on us."

"I thought you liked it when people watched."

"Correction. *I* like to watch, don't get it mixed up. The only person I want watching you is me."

I like the sound of that. *A lot.*

"Joey," I say, leaning over. "Do you want kids one day?"

He gently sets his hand on my cheek. "No."

I didn't expect a yes, but I also wasn't expecting a no.

"You aren't pregnant, are you?"

"No, no, I'm on birth control. That will not be happening."

"Good."

I bite my lip.

"You're great with kids, and you love your brother's kids."

"Because they're *not mine*. Why would you choose to bring a kid into this world? I don't, and I never plan to. That's Keir's choice. He knows what that means, that the kids will eventually take over for him. I would never allow that."

"How can you say that when you're a part of this world?" The car slows to a stop at Lucas' bar. A few other cars are already here.

"This world is fucked-up. Marriage is where I draw the line." He pauses and looks at me curiously, probably wondering why the hell I'm asking him this. Especially now. "Do you want kids?"

I don't know how to answer that, so I say, "No."

"Good, so we're on the same path." He opens his door. "I do love dogs, though. Let's get some dogs." He shuts the door, then walks around to mine and helps me out. When I'm standing, he pulls me to him. "You do like animals, yes? Tell me you aren't a cat person..."

"I'm not a cat person," I manage to reply, swallowing roughly. I need to enjoy this night and him.

"Phew, missed a bullet with that one."

"You're here," Sailor says, walking over to us. She kisses Joey on the cheek before she brings me in for a hug. "Sister... I can call you that, right?"

I look to Joey, who just smirks.

"Sure."

"Good. I've always wanted a sister. Now I have one."

I don't mention that I already have one as we go inside.

It's dark with only a few family members and their partners and some other people I don't know. Maybe twenty people in total, and most are at the bar. Chanel is dressed as Marilyn Monroe, and Lucas is behind her, his hand on her hip.

"I'm so sorry to hear about the bookstore." I turn to see Merci, dressed as Catwoman, in a full leather suit and cat ears, and a man next to her who I'm guessing is supposed to be Batman.

"Same, thank you."

"I heard they may have a lead on who might have done it."

This is news to me.

I haven't really been asking many questions since Becca's death, being too preoccupied trying to get over the loss. So I haven't really had time to process losing the store. The loss of her consumed me, and Joey let it.

"This is Chanel's brother, Brody." I smile and offer my hand, but my mind isn't on him.

What is the lead? I want to know.

Excusing myself, I walk over to Joey, who is sitting at the bar with Keir, their heads leaned in as they speak quietly to one another. When I'm next to Joey, he reaches for me automatically and pulls me between his legs. Keir only stops for a second before he continues in a hushed voice.

"Piper searched his place, and she didn't find much. Everything he had, he kept on his phone." I have absolutely no idea what they're talking about, and I don't interrupt. Joey reaches for his drink and offers it to me. I take it, sipping, as I wait for them to finish speaking. Keir finally gets up and leaves after I've finished two drinks listening in on something I have no idea about.

"Do you want to dance?" he whispers in my ear before he leaves a soft kiss on my neck.

"Do you plan to fuck me in this bunny suit

anytime soon?" I question him back, tilting my head as I look up at him.

"Every which way to Sunday." He groans, lavishing another kiss behind my ear.

"Good, because I wore it for that sole purpose."

"You didn't have to wear something to get me to fuck you. I thought we had established that I will fuck you no matter what." He nips at my ear, then gets off the stool and pulls me out to the dance floor. We're the only ones out here, but he doesn't seem to mind. Our bodies are locked, joined together as one as we rock.

"I'm falling in love with you, Joey."

"I've already fallen, Mrs. Rossi."

THIRTY-THREE

JOEY

Soon, I plan to tear that bunny suit off her with my teeth. Well, that's the plan. She's currently swaying her hips with Chanel as I sit on the sideline and watch.

"Do you think she wants to fuck her?" Lucas asks, stepping up next to me.

"What?" I don't even bother looking at him.

"Your wife. Do you think because she likes pussy too that she wants to fuck my girl?" I turn to look at him and see a serious expression on his face.

"No, they're just dancing, dickhead."

"When you danced with her, did you want to fuck her?" he asks.

"Yes, I want to fuck her all the time."

"My point." He walks over to where the girls are,

and they stop dancing when he reaches them. I watch as his mouth moves and Adora's head falls back, and she starts laughing. Chanel's face goes bright red, and she pushes Lucas away.

He walks back over to me, lifts his drink in his hand, and smiles.

"What did you say?" I ask. Adora is still laughing, and Chanel is completely red-faced.

"I said to Adora, *'You can't fuck her because she's mine. So don't even think about putting any of those pussy moves on her.'*"

"Oh my God, Lucas."

He shrugs as I shake my head. "What, just stating facts."

"My wife does not want to fuck yours."

"Yeah, yeah. Have you seen my girl? I don't make her call me daddy for no good reason."

"Fuck, Lucas, I don't want to hear about what you make her call you in the bedroom."

"Why? I'm happy to share."

"I'm not."

He nudges my shoulder with his. "Come on, tell me how Adora likes it. Is there a secret? I mean, you must at least be good at eating her pussy."

"Lucas," I warn.

"Okay. I know what size your cock is, and it's big."

"How the fuck do you know what size my cock is?"

"I've seen you piss." Of course, he has. "The point is... your big-ass cock must be hitting all those right spots."

"*Oh, porca puttana.*"

"Yeah, for fuck's sake is right." The doors open and Lucas shuts up as he looks in that direction, then he hands me his drink and walks over to whoever is it that's entered. I watch as he speaks to them before Keir is waved over. I should join them, but I'm here to watch my wife dance, which is exactly what she's doing.

Shaking her perfect little fucking ass.

She catches me looking and smiles before she walks over to me, wraps her arms around my shoulders, and leans in to kiss me. Kissing her is one of my favorite things, but her pussy is by far my *absolute favorite thing*.

When she pulls back, she smiles before spinning on her heel and strutting back to Chanel.

"Joey." I turn to see Keir behind me. He nods to the back room where Lucas has gone and wants me to follow him. I don't want to go with him because I am perfectly happy where I am, watching Adora smile and laugh and shake her ass. I like seeing her happy. But like a good little soldier, I get up and follow Keir into the back room where there is a one-way mirror in the middle of one wall.

"Joey," Lucas says. I turn around but stay near the mirror. "You need to hear this."

"Make it fast."

"Joey, you are not to do anything stupid, do you understand?" Keir warns, which means this has something to do with Adora.

I eye him suspiciously.

"Would you listen if I said that about Sailor?" I ask, but he doesn't answer me. "I figured as much."

"It's a command, Joey. Stay calm."

"I am calm. But you're all making me real fucking antsy." I turn back to the mirror to watch her dancing. Merci has joined them on the dance floor, and Sailor is drinking shots at the bar. It's going to be a fun night for Keir when he gets back out there.

Facing Keir again, I nod to Sailor. "Your wife has had three shots since I've been standing here."

"Fucking hell." He looks at Lucas. "I'll be back. Stay fucking put and wait for me."

Lucas nods as he walks out.

I nod my head to the man sitting next to Lucas

and follow with, "Who's that?"

"My informant." Lucas smiles. The man sits there holding a bottle of water and looking everywhere but at me.

"What does he know?"

"Keir isn't back yet." I look out to see Keir pick Sailor up and throw her over his shoulder before he walks back in here, shuts the door behind him, and places her in a chair. He goes to Lucas' bar refrigerator and grabs a bottle of water, then hands it to her. "Drink this."

"Drink your cock," she barks back, then giggles. "Or I can."

He groans, and Lucas laughs.

We wait a few minutes while Sailor drinks her water and crosses her arms and looks around. "What's the meeting for?" Her eyes pin to the man in here with us. "And why wasn't I invited if he's in here?" She points to him as Keir walks behind her and places his hands on her shoulder, then nods to Lucas.

"Go."

I glance around to see all eyes on me.

"I'm about to kill your wife," Lucas says simply, and I act on impulse alone, pulling my gun and aiming it at him.

"Joey," Keir warns.

"You will not touch her."

Lucas taps the man sitting in front of him, fear written all over the guy's face. "Talk."

"Scott wants her back. She is legally married to him." Everything in me freezes. "The shop was her first warning," he adds. "The second will be her sister being sent back in pieces."

"She is *my* wife. You're telling lies." I'm shaking my head as he pulls out a piece of paper. Leaning in, I see a young Adora, dressed in a white dress, with a man wearing a tuxedo. But the one thing that stands out immediately is not her dress, or even the man. It's her belly.

"She was pregnant."

"He has their child."

I look up from the photograph, my gun still aimed at Lucas. "You will *not* kill her," I bark at Lucas, and the motherfucker doesn't even flinch.

"She's lied, deceived her way in. For all we know, she could be working with some of the older families who hold a grudge against Keir for killing his father."

Fuck.

Fuck.

Fuck.

"You don't know that." *This can't be happening.*

"I wouldn't even have told you. I would have just killed her, but Keir wanted you to know first."

I turn to Sailor and Keir.

Sailor leans over and throws up all over her expensive shoes while Keir only nods.

"You made me marry her. You made me love her. To what? To tell me it was all a lie?" I ask him, seething. If blood boils, the evidence is currently rushing through my veins.

"I didn't know it was a lie."

"Fuck you," I shout and pull the trigger. The bullet hits Lucas' informant right between the eyes, and his head lulls forward and smashes into the table, covering Lucas in blood.

Sailor throws up again.

Keir rubs her back, shaking his head at me.

"You can't have her," I say firmly, my eyes locked on Keir's, but they're only seeing red.

"She is married to someone else, Joey. Has had someone else's baby."

"This is the first time you've heard of this?" I ask him, reaffirming as my head spins.

Keir nods. "First, just now."

Lucas is swearing when I look back at him. "This suit was expensive."

"It's a normal suit."

"Still expensive. I was trying to be a mob boss. How did I do?" Lucas asks, and if it were up to me, I'd kill him next for not shutting the fuck up.

"Shit," Keir says answering Lucas' stupid question.

"Damn," Lucas says, sighing. "But now I have the blood. That counts, right?"

"None of this is helping me," I growl out the words that I don't want to say.

"Don't let them do it, Joey. Please don't," Sailor whispers.

Keir looks at her but doesn't listen.

Liar.

I never thought I would think that of my wife.

A liar.

What else has she hidden from me?

A child.

That's not a small feat to hide either.

"Give me five with her."

"That's all you'll get," Keir says, and Sailor stands up to yell at him.

I get moving instantly, not a moment to waste as I throw the door open with a bang, my eyes scanning the room for Adora. I don't find her on the dance floor with Chanel, so I stalk over to Chanel to ask her where she is. Her eyes widen as she takes in my crazed expression.

"Where did she go?"

"Outside. A man wanted to talk to her." She nods to the door we came in earlier, her brow furrowing. I go straight outside to find her getting into a car. This is the part where I should raise my gun, but my arms are stuck to my sides as I watch her slide in. She looks back, half in and half out of the car.

"I'm sorry." She mouths the words to me as she closes herself inside, and I watch in shock as the car drives off. Leaving me standing there confused, hurt, and furious. Looking down on the ground, I find her ring on the sidewalk and my chest clenches. Picking it up, I slide it onto my pinkie finger as the door opens and Keir steps out.

"Where is she?" he asks, looking up and down the street.

"Gone," I tell him, staring at the ring on my finger.

"You let her go?"

"I did."

"You know you'll have to find her now and kill them both."

I swallow hard, nodding. "I do."

"Sooner rather than later, Joey."

The 'Nice' Brother

We hear betrayal has a middle name, and it starts
with A for Adora.
Will her husband do what's asked of him?
Which love will win?
The one born of family...
... or the one of wife?

WANT MORE OF JOEY? ARRANGED
HEARTS IS BOOK 2

FIRST CHAPTER OF UNLIKELY QUEEN

His touch brands my very soul. I can feel it all the way down to the depths of my bones. It's like a fire licking at its victim and being drenched in ice water at the same time. His lips touch mine, branding me, marking my soul so anyone and everyone can see or feel it.

I am his.

In this moment and forever, I belong to him.

It feels like I'm in a daze. I shouldn't know what he's doing, but somehow, I know every single detail. It's like a puzzle in my head, working it out, putting it together piece by piece.

A sweep of his tongue, and the fire smolders.

A bite of my lip, and the fire burns brighter.

My insides are shaking, not understanding but wanting as much as he can give to quench my insatiable need for him.

He pulls back, and in an instant, everything changes. I'm not blind. I can see clearly. His eyes shine brightly into mine, silver and steady. It feels like a drug is clearing from my system, cleansing me of him. I crave his intoxication once more—a hit—that one single touch or a single look can give.

"You feel it, don't you?" My eyes close at the sound of his voice, and I shiver as it takes on an edge. "Now I need you to run... run as if your life depends on it. Because if you don't, I will find you, and I will take you."

Is it a malicious promise or a delicious threat? What I do know is that it's one I delight in.

"The prophecy?" I ask, and he nods in answer, wings expanding out in all their glory.

And I find myself craving him once more.

"If it comes true..." he continues by way of warning, "...our worlds will intertwine. You will have more power than anyone could ever dream of, and no one will be able to stop you."

"You won't touch me again?"

I miss it already—his touch, his taste.

"I won't be able to." His lips meet my cheek, then the same words whisper once more in my ear. "Run, little fighter. Run."

AVAILABLE NOW!

ABOUT THE AUTHOR

USA Today Best Selling Author T.L. Smith loves to write her characters with flaws so beautiful and dark you can't turn away. Her books have been translated into several languages. If you don't catch up with her in her home state of Queensland, Australia you can usually find her travelling the world, either sitting on a beach in Bali or exploring Alcatraz in San Francisco or walking the streets of New York.

ALSO BY T.L SMITH

Connect with T.L Smith by tlsmithauthor.com